TO HELL AND GONE IN TEXAS

RUSS HALL

To Hell and Gone in Texas
A Red Adept Publishing Book

Red Adept Publishing, LLC
104 Bugenfield Court
Garner, NC 27529
http://RedAdeptPublishing.com/

First Print Edition: August 2014
ISBN-13: 978-1-940215-33-4 (Red Adept Publishing)
ISBN-10: 1-940215-33-1

Cover and Formatting: Streetlight Graphics

The most precious thing in life is its uncertainty. Leaving something incomplete makes it interesting and gives one the feeling that there is room for growth.

—Kenko, 14th Century Japan

CHAPTER ONE

THE BODIES LAY TWISTED, ONE caught in the act of running, the other on his knees, either begging or because he had been ordered there. The wide pools of blood had begun to turn the brown of a worn, sun-baked saddle. Vultures, both black ones and turkey buzzards, lined the limbs of surrounding trees, a few circling above as they rode a thermal. Their pattern had led the passing deputy to the discovery. Clayton looked at the bare limbs of the old dead pecan tree near the double-wide house where the biggest bunch of them had perched, waiting. The two kinds of Texas buzzard didn't always get along. The turkey buzzards were bigger, but the black buzzards were more social, and as a group, they usually ran off the more solitary turkey buzzards, unless there promised to be enough to eat for all.

"Another one over here, Sheriff!" Deputy Wayon Gallard bent over the body, staring closely at the bled-out stump of neck between the shoulders.

Wayon knew not to touch anything, so Sheriff Harold Clayton said nothing. All the words he might want to say had been sucked right out of him. He'd been at his job a goodish spell, but every once in a while, he opened a rotten egg of a case, and the current one promised to be an ostrich egg. The media hadn't caught wind of it yet. That was about the only thing he had going for him so far.

He had Bob Simmons, the first deputy on the scene, to thank for having the sense to call him at home.

He'd been halfway through a plate of fresh biscuits smothered in dried-beef gravy when the call came. Mary Lou, bless her southern-fried heart, only made the dish for him once every two or three weeks. She worked harder at keeping his sodium intake and blood pressure down than he did. Still, his day was shaping up better than it had for the three men they had found so far.

Clayton looked up at the cloudless, flat, pale blue slate of a sky that, aside from the circling vultures, was empty. It was a good day to be doing pretty much anything else. The air felt heavy, solid and still. He looked at the nearest trees—live oaks and pecans— only the tiniest scrap of breeze moving the leaves on the uppermost limbs. Down where he stood, the field was absent of sound, pensive.

Clayton walked over to where Wayon stood beside the third corpse. The splatter of the arterial spray said it had happened there. At least there wasn't a crime scene somewhere else where the guys had been dragged from.

The last decapitation he'd seen in person—not in an M.E.'s photos after the fact—was a young woman who'd died in an auto accident. He had been driving home from his office and just happened to pull over at the scene before the first responders had even arrived. She'd been texting and driving. The cell phone was still clutched in her smashed hand. Her neck was a solid smear of fresh blood where the broken edge of the windshield had crashed through her neck.

In the case of the body in front of him, a sharp object— machete probably—had done the job. He could see the top of the severed spine and the dried ends of veins. One minute, each had had a head, and the next not. Clean, professional work. He looked at the way the blades of tall grass had been bent and broken in places. The crime scene unit could make more sense of it than he could. He was still deciding when to call them in.

His very first exposure to "protect and serve" had come as playground monitor in elementary school, so long ago that he hated even to put a date on it. The other kids might have thought "snitch," but he'd been a big enough boy that none of them were brave enough to say so. His main role was preventing anyone from being a bully and seeing that no one got hurt, or being the first one there if they did. Maybe the vice principal and teacher who'd nominated him—invested him with that curse of an honor—had done so to keep him from being a bully himself. They were probably right to task him with protecting others. He'd come to think of the playground as his turf, and he had the kind of toughness combined with youthful zeal that could have gone either way.

The job had been easy enough for him, very little to do except catch the occasional peek up a flying skirt as he passed the swing sets. His moment of distinction came when he reported a car that had parked close to the playground on three days in one week. The cops who swooped in on the car probably expected—as Clayton did—they would find some crusty geezer with binoculars. Instead, they hauled in two up-and-coming local entrepreneurs looking to expand their territories with half a kilo of Maui Wowie under the seats. Clayton had gotten enough credit for his involvement in the bust to feel he had protected the playground against just the kind of outside influence that always sought to encroach, to inveigle its way into the lives of innocent people. It gave him a taste he hadn't been able to shake.

As an adult, he protected the playground of Travis County, over a thousand square miles smack dab in the middle of Texas. The land sat astride the Balcones Fault, between the Edwards Plateau to the west and the Blackland Prairie over toward where the sun rose. The county was a bit bigger than that gravel-covered playground lot, and had well over a million people to protect, many of them, though certainly not all, nearly as innocent as those school kids of his youth. Most neither knew nor even sensed the forces outside their secure little world that threatened to intrude on their lives to take the whole lot of them out on a fast bus to the other side of nowhere.

Wayon pushed the front brim of his hat up an inch. "Who the hell takes a head?"

Clayton held up a hand, trying to think. How would he have done it? And, okay, why? The wind picked up and swept through the tops of the trees in the surrounding copses of woods. Cottonwoods stood along the far creek, mesquite and mountain cedar ran up the hillsides, and live oak, post oak, and the one stately, old denuded pecan crowding the house. The tall grass in the surrounding field bent and swayed in the breeze. *Folks think they live all the hell of the way out here in bumfart nowhere that they're away from it all, insulated. T'ain't so these days.*

"What do you suppose happened to the heads?" Wayon knelt on one knee, careful to stay clear from the blood and any possible footprints. "I didn't see them laying around anywhere."

This body wore the same sort of jeans, boots, and worn shirt with pearl buttons as the other two, but the backs of the hands showed wrinkles, pronounced veins, and one or two liver spots. Clayton bent closer. Yep. The old man. The other two would be his boys. He straightened and glanced toward the house: a double-wide on a cement slab, two pickups parked in front, one red, one white, both Fords that had seen a lot of tough living and rough roads.

The license plates above the trailer hitches were dented inward and scarred from trailer tongues gouging them during stops and turns until they were nearly unreadable. Those trucks sure must have been hauling around some stuff they shouldn't have.

To drive his vehicle in past the gate, Clayton had used a bolt cutter on the padlocked chain. No one had gone out that way, unless they had locked up after themselves, which wasn't likely. He looked around a little more, wondering which way they'd come in and how they'd left. There sure were a lot of empty open spaces to land a helicopter. Whoever had done that would have had to get in and get out. None of the bodies held weapons. Maybe they'd been expecting something else. Not this. A fly buzzed atop one of the corpses, its noise seeming as loud as a jetliner.

Clayton sighed and straightened. "Well, guess we got no choice here. Bob was right to make the call. But we gotta get the crime scene guys out here. Better get Mel out here, too. Gonna be another damn media shit storm." Mel Kawle was the PIO—public information officer. Clayton didn't like to call him out on a Sunday, and he knew Mel's daughter was having a birthday. Mel would grump, but he'd come. Best he get on it early.

Past the house, two black vans were coming down the road, heading his way fast. *Well, crap!* His stomach gave a lurch that even the corpses hadn't managed to cause. He should have stayed to finish those biscuits and gravy, gone long cold by now. How the hell did those guys get wind of this? He sure as Sam Houston had better not find out that any of his men had called them, or someone would find himself patrolling the far outreaches of the toughest part of the county. The mess took on a whole deeper stench if those damned ICE guys were in any way involved.

Simmons was posted at the end of the drive. He waved

the vans through. Clayton watched the approaching vans, standing straight and tall for someone pushing seventy hard. He was what they called in this part of Texas a good ol' boy—John Wayne-big and imposing, with a track record for integrity unsullied in spite of holding a regularly contested political office. He was liked, or at least accepted, by most of his constituents and popular enough to win no matter who they put up against him, most people having noticed he had come to have a mother-hen affection for his county. *His county, dammit.*

The Texas sun had gotten an early jump on heating up the morning, but Clayton felt pretty sure that wasn't what put the sudden patina of sweat on his forehead under the brim of his hat or what probably showed as a flush on his cheeks. His heart pumped double-time, and the resulting heat rushed all the way from his toes to his temples.

Wayon stared up at him. "You okay?"

"Yeah, I'm fine. Just peachy keen. Dandy." Mary Lou liked to say Clayton was most always as calm and cool as the center seed in a low-hanging cucumber. She should see him now, his insides boiling and hands tightening into fists until he made them stop.

Wayon started to respond then stopped himself, showing the potential for growing wisdom. For the space of seven seconds, Clayton could smell the aroma of the fresh pot of French Roast coffee and the warm biscuits as he'd poured on the gravy—what he'd put aside to be here. He could see the blue Delft plates on the red-and-white-checked tablecloth and didn't know why that irritated as much as comforted him. Then he was back outside in the growing heat of a morning that had all the promise of becoming a wormy grape.

The vans pulled up. Jaime Avila stepped out of the first, not a tall man but a solid one. He had a strut to his stride, along with an eagerness that not many people would show when approaching a crime scene this ugly. His black ball cap had three letters across the front: ICE. Immigration and Customs Enforcement. Two other men, also dressed in black, got out of the front van and leaned on the side, waiting. The second van would be Jaime's own crime scene crew.

Clayton felt the smoldering embers in his gut grow into small flames no amount of antacid could stave off. In all his years of law enforcement—his personal life too, for that matter—Clayton had believed in taking care of his own business, cleaning up his own messes, no matter how cluttered. Ask anyone. The thing about agencies like ICE was they didn't always ask, nicely or at all. They were just there, suddenly, and in charge. If you had a beef, you could take it up with the Department of Homeland Security, something that didn't exist for most of the early part of Clayton's career.

The bigger question pressing him was one he doubted he'd get answered. Just what the hell was Jaime doing close enough to be here so Johnny-on-the-spot, and with his own crime scene crew along for the ride?

Clayton reached into his pockets and felt to see if he'd thought to slip in a roll of antacid tablets. Nope. His hand slid over his service piece holster that held his Glock 17, the leather worn from years of use. He'd slipped the belt on even though he wore his "at home on Sunday" clothes: jeans, boots, and a dark blue polo shirt. His fingers lingered on the belt, slid along the smooth leather as polished from wear as the holster. For a second, the belt felt slick. He realized it was his fingertips that were moist.

On any given day, Clayton's three hundred deputies and nine hundred correction facility employees, as well as its tactical and investigation teams, ran under the guidance of separate captains reporting to Clayton. He had a chief deputy, three majors, and eight captains working under him. Only when something really quirky came along had he asked his men to call so he could step to the front himself and seek to contain the situation. The county had a robust crime element that had tried pretty much everything and was always looking to get into the next latest fad. "Contain" also meant handle the media. He couldn't muzzle them, but he could work with them. That crowd with their overzealous roving reporters and camera crews out was eager to compete, stir things up, and grab all those advertising dollars. They were the hyenas to the kill.

Sundays were usually his day of reflection and personal peace. Still, Simmons had been right to call him. Yet his toes were about to be stepped on, and he was going to have to grin and act as though he liked it. Well, he'd be double-damned if he would enjoy it. He had never sought to be some despotic ruler, but it frosted his pumpkin when some federal agency butted in and yanked *his county* away from him. He couldn't quite muster a smile for the approaching ICE man, but he did manage not to look ready to bite.

Jaime came up to them and looked down at the headless, bled-out corpse. "Do you know who they are?"

Clayton pointed. "This one's Hank Collier. Senior. One of those over there is Hank Junior. The other's his brother Seth."

"You're sure?"

"They still have fingers. We'll run the prints to confirm." Clayton could feel his sentences getting shorter, but he concentrated on staying civil.

Jaime had to tilt his head back to look up at Clayton. "That's okay. I'll turn my crew loose... if that's okay with you?" It had not been a request, rather a statement of how things would be. The taut skin of his face—toasted the brown of a roasted chestnut—made him look youthful. His shoulders—broad for his height—helped him look fit, and his brisk pace made him seem eager, maybe a little too eager. "I hear your best detective has retired anyway. Let us handle this. We'll keep you in the front end of the loop."

Clayton didn't say anything.

Jaime cocked his head a bit more. "You're the only big county sheriff I know who would come out himself to get a first take on something that might turn out to be a bigger threat than usual. You should be sitting behind that desk, thinking about budgets, politics, and things that come in fast from the corner of your vision."

"This was one of those."

"There you go. You see? And with this one here, I'm all ready to help you with that." Jaime's grin showed white teeth that had cost him a fair bit of money.

Clayton, despite feeling the flames in his gut shoot upward three feet, managed to speak in a calm tone. "Do you have some idea what this is about?" He waved a hand at the bodies.

"I'm afraid I do." Jaime stared down at the nearest body. "I couldn't have stopped it. No telling where this will happen next."

"You were awful handy."

Jaime shrugged. "I get hunches." His words came out as olive oil being poured over a warmed smooth stone, but that didn't make anything he said easier for Clayton to stomach.

The thing about the ICE bunch was they took, took, and took every scrap of intel they could get from a department like Clayton's. But trying to get anything back from them was like trying to wrestle a pearl from a deepwater clam.

9

"Should we be very worried?" Clayton ached to reach up and rub at a trickle of sweat running out from under his hat down his temple, but he fought back the urge.

"No need for you to fret. This is something we can tend to for you. You know, I suspect those who did this are done here. But they have more to do elsewhere."

"Where do you expect them next?"

"That, I can't tell you. I wish to hell I knew." Jaime glanced at the house then back to the nearest body. "These men here"—he waved a hand toward the headless corpses—"do they have rap sheets?"

"Short piddly ones. Hank Senior was a cut-up back in his day, fights and such. The three of them, him and his two sons, tried to start up a meth lab once, a while back. Not enough chemistry smarts among them to make paste. Then they were quiet awhile but seemed to have money. Hard to tell what they were up to."

"That fits the pattern."

"What pattern's that?"

"You let me worry about that. It's not likely to happen again in your turf. This one here's barely in your county at all."

"I wish it was to hell and gone into someone else's county altogether." Clayton paused. "Any idea what happened to their heads? Why take them?"

"Maybe they're trying to make a point. Or maybe they collect. I've heard of worse."

"I imagine you have."

"Look, we were following a lead that brought us here, if that's what's putting the bunch in your shorts. You don't have a leak in your precious department. Don't let that worry you."

Clayton nodded, lips tight together.

"Now, if you don't mind, I'd like to get my men to work before... well, it's getting hot. You'll get my report."

"Knock yourselves out. I got plenty of other stuff on my plate. Just make sure I get every detail." Clayton knew that was too much to expect. He hated, hated, hated vagueness, but that was what he was going to get. *This was his county, dammit.*

"You sure this is something that belongs on your plate?" Clayton asked, in spite of intending not to do so.

"Look at it. Does it look like your everyday run-of-the-mill thing? Hell, it's why you're out here and not the rest of your people yet." Jaime waved a dismissive hand, turned, and walked off. His men were pouring out of the second van and coming toward him.

"Just another damn case. Good thing it's someone else's mess," Clayton muttered, trying hard to sell it to himself but not succeeding at all.

The only way to stay on top of a county was to know everything, and he sure as Stephen F. Austin wasn't going to get that kind of granular detail from these guys. The only silver lining he could see was that there would be no publicity with Jaime's bunch, though Clayton would have to deal with kin, not a big deal in this instance—just a couple of ticked-off ex-wives, neither of whom had seen an alimony check in many a moon. Hell, the murders might even be good news to them. Still, it pissed him to the ragged edges of his tired soul not to be able to do his own stinking job.

Clayton took out his phone and started punching in the number to call off his crime scene crew. He stopped, realizing he hadn't called them in yet. Well, he had one more call to make, to his former detective, the one Jaime thought was so damn good, who was probably out fishing and enjoying life, something Clayton was beginning to realize he'd forgotten how to do.

CHAPTER TWO

THE LINE SLICED THROUGH THE water as Al Quinn reeled faster. The minute the fish saw the boat, it dove and might have pulled Al out of the front chair if he hadn't stood and lowered the rod tip, to let it run. When his cell phone rang, he transferred the rod to one hand and glanced at his cell's screen. *Damn.*

As the fish surged, pulling against his reel's drag, he punched the Talk button and put the phone to his ear. He tried to hold it there with his shoulder, but that never worked well. "What?"

"You do know who's calling you, don't you?" Clayton's voice was louder than usual, his "upset about something but not going to show it" tone.

"I know I've got a real bucket mouth on the line. I mean at the end of my fishing line. Can this wait? If you're going to ask if I can help with something, a little investigating favor, the answer's probably no."

"Don't flatter yourself. You know us. We clean our own messes."

"Then what's up? Did Mary Lou burn the toast or something? Hemorrhoids kicking up?" Al imagined he heard the sound of Clayton's molars rubbing together like a mill grinding wheat.

"No."

"Okay. What is it then?" Al heard distant voices on

the line—shouts—though it was Sunday, when Clayton should have been home.

Crime scene? He knew about Clayton's standing request for the deputies to call him in if anything smelled or looked funny. Al had been along on a few of those himself. Maybe that was what was putting sand in Clayton's craw. If that was it, he probably had Wayon, the up-and-comer, along. They didn't need Al.

"It's your brother," Clayton said.

"What about him? You know how it is with us."

"Al, I got the message earlier this morning. I've been up to my ears since, or I'd have called sooner. He's in a hospital. City homicide is looking into it as a possible."

"Homicide? They think someone tried to kill Maury?" It had been a long while since Al had even said the name.

"I don't know what they think. I'm just giving you the head's up."

"Well... thanks, I guess."

Clayton clicked off.

What the hell was that? Al felt a niggle of disappointment that the department hadn't been asking for his help. It had been only a short while since he'd been a part of all that—the pursuit, the unraveling, the working as a team. Yet it seemed a long time since he'd felt a part of anything, connected to the world at all. He told himself he was adjusting to being alone and that he quite liked it. Yeah, he was eating up that hollow, unattached feeling. He didn't need to ask permission if he wanted to go fishin', as Tom Waits once put it.

Al went back to work on getting what promised to be a good bass into the boat. She was trying her best to pull the line toward a tree limb hanging down into the water. *Only damn bit of structure along the whole shoreline and she was trying to tangle him up in it. Figures.* He started to

13

raise his rod tip to turn her head while he reeled in line. Instead, he relaxed and lowered the rod, on purpose. If he gave her that much slack, she could scoot in half a whip of a lamb's tail. A quick shake of the fish's head, and he felt the line go empty. He started to reel in the lure.

One reason he headed out onto the lake after a rough day was that just being on the water soaked up whatever was gnawing at him. Bouncing gently on the wakes of other passing boats, breathing the moist air, and casting away calmed him to his core. Catching fish was a bonus, didn't even have to happen. Back when he'd worked for the department, he'd come home from one of those draining, gut-wrenching days, and the reflection rippling off the surface settled his mind and charged his batteries. But the magic of it had faded at the moment. He felt as hollow and empty as a dried gourd. He stowed away the rod then went around to get behind the console.

Maury. He sure hadn't thought about his brother much lately—on purpose. He fired up the boat then surprised himself by going in a lot faster than he'd come out. He guessed he could at least see what trouble the fathead had gotten into. Then again, maybe he wouldn't go, shouldn't go. Still, he found himself inching the throttle forward until the boat's motor roared louder as cool water misted his face.

———◆———

As he pulled up to the dock behind his house, a blue heron rose from the shoreline where it had been fishing and, with an irritated loud squawk, flapped its long wings. The bird headed across the water, looking for a new spot to stand. At least there was still enough water in the lake for Al to back off on the motor and give a short last second pop of the reverse to ease his boat into place. If the drought kept up much longer, he was going to need to spend some money to extend the rails that let the dock slide down to stay on the lake's surface.

Al bent over and saw that he had about another eighteen inches of rail left. *Come on, rain.* The grass just above the rocky shore had turned a yellowed brown. That reminded him. He needed to swing by the feed store and get more deer food. Handy place on his way into Austin— he just drove through, and they threw a couple of bags in the back of his truck. His hunter friends told him the deer they'd harvested in the woods had been showing ribs with their stomachs full of cedar, a last resort for starving deer. The regular herd that visited Al's house daily would be swinging through soon. No one had said it was up to him to keep them alive through the drought, but he had started feeding them, and they had come to expect it. He looked along the shore but didn't see any of them yet.

He tied the boat, front and sides, put his tackle in the shed, and secured the padlock on the door. He walked up the path to what his friends called his "man cave" of a home. Two stories of rustic-looking wood covered the outside, but he had spent the first six weeks of his retirement refurbishing the kitchen and master bedroom and bathroom until the inside was the way he'd pictured it in his head. He didn't give a whoop about the outside. Burglaries by boat happened to houses on the waterfront, and he'd just as soon his place didn't look like a good target. He always kept it locked tight, though, just in case.

His house, his sanctuary. He spent way too much time alone. He knew that, but he had come to love and crave the solitude.

The house had been built on a hill. Usually thick with grass and wildflowers, the lack of rain had made the slopes on either side turn the same tired brownish yellow of all

15

the other stressed and dying vegetation. Mesquite, scrub elm, post oak, and live oak trees grew thick enough around the house to nearly obscure it from the lake, except where the upper deck looked out over the water. The back door downstairs opened into the lower level of the house, while upstairs the front door opened to a higher ground level.

He usually went up and turned on the classical music station as soon as he was home. This time Al stayed downstairs for a moment, crossed what had from time to time been a guest room, and pushed open the door to the laundry room. He reached up to the shelf above the washing machine and turned on his police scanner. Some would call him nosy, but he had an itch to know just what it was that had Clayton out working on a Sunday. It must be something darn juicy for the man to take so long to pass the information along to Al in the afternoon when Clayton had heard about Maury in the morning.

The scanner took a few moments to warm up. He kept it tuned to the Austin/Travis County P25 trunked system set on the 453.7 frequency. There was no reason for him to even have it since he was no longer active, except for moments like this.

He listened for a few minutes to the routine chatter of dispatchers and deputies. There was no mention of Clayton being in the field himself or working something big enough for him to be so distracted and irritable. That only confirmed Al's suspicion that something was up, but he doubted that the business with Maury had anything to do with that.

⋘◆⋙

A growing, whirring roar swept across Lake Buchanan, a body of water in the chain comprised of a series of dammed lakes on the former Colorado River that wound

16

through central Texas, heading down toward Austin. The helicopter flew from south to north, low enough to cast a large dark shadow on the water and whip the surface into a white-capped wake. Just before it rose over a stand of mountain cedar that dotted the climbing side of a mesa ahead, three objects fell toward the water.

A fisherman up the mouth of a feeder creek was out of sight as the three heads hit the water with identical splashes. They sank almost as quickly as they'd fallen from the sky into thirty feet of brown water.

CHAPTER THREE

A L STEPPED OUT OF THE elevator and got directions at the nurses' station from a stocky, blond, curly-haired woman in pink scrubs. She looked busy enough to be the only nurse on the floor. The worry lines on her tanned face contrasted with her patient smile. Her eyes hinted that she might even be capable of amusement if she weren't in such a hurry. Her name tag read, "Bonnie." As soon as she'd answered his question, she grabbed a clipboard and hustled down the hallway in the opposite direction.

The room he wanted was right down the hall, third doorway on the right. Music poured through the open doorway. The bed by the window was empty, its screen pulled back and the sheets taut across the mattress.

Al glanced up at the TV mounted high on the wall. An orchestra was playing. He eased closer to the occupied bed and leaned down. *Good lord!*

The man's hair was thick and full, though going to silver much more than the speckle of grey at Al's temples. The skin was lighter around the eyes, probably from wearing sunglasses by a pool. The complexion was tanned, darkly tanned, almost cooked into a patina of brown, but with the deep wrinkled lines of a walnut. The man's flesh was loose at the neck, like that of someone who spent a great deal of time glancing behind him, a hare one step ahead of the hounds. An oxygen tube ran to his nose, and an IV line lead from a nearly empty pouch to one arm. The sheet-covered body looked frail and as lean as an emaciated strip of jerky—bones held together by sinew and little more. A skeleton waiting for the next step.

"Not sure that's your brother, Al?" someone asked from behind him.

Al turned to the woman in the doorway. "I don't know, Fergie. I suppose so."

"What do you mean 'You suppose so'? That is Maury... isn't it?" Detective Ferguson Jergens peered at him like a scientist peering into a Petri dish. She wore her red hair long. Her eyes rarely blinked. She was, at six foot two, taller than his five feet eleven and looked more like she ought to be modeling on a runway rather than handling investigations.

It had been a long time since he'd asked her to prom. She'd been gangly and a bit of a nerd then. Well, a lot of a nerd. Maury had chided him at the time, as if Al wasn't already headed toward what was going to be one of the most memorably bad evenings of his life. "A girl that tall, well, when you're nose to nose, your toes are in it; when you're toes to toes, your nose is in it." Maury had been a class act even then.

Nothing he'd said to Al was worse than the event itself. The picture her parents took of them—her skinny and towering over him like a broom handle with a face, him looking at those string-like straps going over her shoulders to hold her dress up, and him just handing her the corsage. And the dancing. Ah, the dancing. She wore high heels, of course. He slid his feet across the dusted wood, being careful not to step on her toes, but not dancing well at all as a consequence. He looked up, and she frowned down at him. He could see straight up her nose. That had been

19

their first and only date. Whoever had done her current makeover ought to get a medal. She compensated for her stunning appearance by never smiling.

"Well?" she said.

He realized he'd been staring at her and cleared his throat as he glanced away. "Well, I haven't seen him or been around him in over twenty years. People change. What happened to him? Why's a detective like yourself involved?" The face in that hospital bed had aged about twice as fast as his own. It hardly seemed possible, but it was his brother.

"It's standard in a case like his."

"What kind of case do you mean?"

"Where there's anything suspicious."

"Like what?"

"Well, the lab tests suggest he'd taken the equivalent of three Viagra tablets. Why do you suppose he'd do that?"

"Ambitious?"

"He had no prescription. I don't think he could have gotten one with his heart. That's why he was in a place like that."

"A place like what? Wasn't it just some sort of rest home?"

"He was frail enough to need the assisted-living accommodations. He had fallen a few times, hurt himself. He was recovering."

"Really? How'd he get so frail?" Al eased close to the one flower arrangement, three yellow roses surrounded by baby's breath and ferns in a red glass bud vase. He opened the small card enough to make out the name: Roma.

"Now you're outside the area of my expertise, or interest. We think someone might've slipped him the pills. If that's what almost killed him, then it's attempted murder."

He let go of the card and turned back to Fergie. "Why

20

did you ask the sheriff to call me? Don't you have a handle on this?"

"What makes you think it was me?"

"You're here, aren't you?"

"Well, for one, you *were* a sheriff's department detective. Homicide at that."

"Retired."

"I'm surprised you didn't wait to get your thirty in."

"Twenty-five was enough. What's your other reason?"

She shrugged. "He's your brother." Her eyes swept over him, giving him a visual pat-down.

"Looking for weapons?"

"It wouldn't be the first time someone showed up looking to finish things off."

"So, now I'm your lead suspect, too?"

"Always have been, Al, with the history between you two. You've done enough of these investigations. First ones we look at are family and friends."

He looked away. Two wispy strings of grey cobwebs hung in the upper corner. They undulated in the current from the air conditioning vent. He panned down to her face again. Her expression grew intense, like a praying mantis for a snack.

"Like I said, Maury and I haven't kept up. Is that why you got the sheriff to let me know? So I'd come here? Do you really think I might be a suspect?"

"Well, you do seem awfully unfazed about his near death. Do you care much one way or the other whether I get to the bottom of this?"

"Oh, I care all right. Maury was a lot of things, but he didn't deserve for someone to try to murder him, if that's the case. Well, not so far as I know. I thought about it often enough myself once. That was a long time ago." He caught her eyes narrowing. "I was far away, have an alibi, and wouldn't have bothered if I could. Time and distance have been all I needed. I never thought I'd see him again. I was wrong about that. I didn't think I'd talk to him again. I was right about that, it seems."

"He's not dead yet." Fergie glanced at Maury. "Word is that you've been gradually withdrawing from life ever since you and your wife split. But that doesn't mean you couldn't have done it."

"Your marriage didn't end in a train wreck like mine."

"You don't know that."

"I guess I don't." He took a deep breath. "You think that no matter what I ought to be there for my brother?"

She pursed her lips into a twist at the corner of her mouth. "Look, in your job you dealt every day with sacrifice, betrayal, and even personal grace under pressure. But none of that seems to have touched you where you live. It's all been occupational, hasn't it?"

The music from the TV grew louder. Fergie stepped into the room and toward it.

"Leave it on." Bonnie stood in the doorway, holding a fresh IV bag. "It does him good, I think. At least it does him no harm."

Al had only glanced at her before. Up close, he could see she stood about five-three, had an upturned nose, couldn't be more than mid-thirties, and had a deep brown tan on her face, arms, and legs. Her bosom pressed tight against her pink scrubs, as did a well-fed, round little belly. She gave them an elfish smile and headed for the bed.

"That's Beethoven's Triple Concerto in C," Al said. "The conductor is Alan Gilbert. Enthusiastic fellow, eh? The violinist is Gil Shaham, the cellist is Yo-Yo Ma, and the pianist is Emanuel Ax."

"And you know this how?" Fergie asked.

He glanced over at her. She had one eyebrow arched and was eyeing him as she switched out the IV bags.

"It's from the one hundred twentieth anniversary of Carnegie Hall. I saw it on PBS." His gaze was drawn back to the television, where the three men were taking solo turns on their instruments.

Emanuel Ax, an older man, played from somewhere deep inside himself on the piano. Yo-Yo Ma closed his eyes when he sawed away at his cello, then opened them at the end of his solo, grinning with delight. He turned his gaze to Gil Shaham, who segued into a violin lead, with Yo-Yo Ma waving in encouragement. The three men were at the top of their game, having a delightful time riding the passion of something about which they cared very much, with all the intensity of their beings.

Al wasn't sure why he couldn't tear his eyes away or what it was he felt inside. *A yearning?*

"Why was Maury staying here?" Al lifted a hand to sweep it across the wall of certificates on the bookshelf above a row of three file cabinets. One worn, black leather-bound copy of *Gray's Anatomy* stood on the shelf next to a purplish-silver vase with a chipped lip. Al thought of the place as a rest home, although the sign out by the road called it a resident nursing home. *Same thing.*

The woman behind the desk, Gladys Willstone, had grey hair going to white that had been cut so short it was a half hop from being a buzz cut. She wore oversized tortoise-shell glasses that turned into mirrors for a second when she reached for one of the files in front of her. One of the plaques on the wall said she had an RN degree. The look she was giving Al said his questions were as enjoyable to her as biting into a rotten quince.

23

"Some of us get older faster than others, whether it's genetics, burning the candle on both ends, or merely a life lived incautiously or too hard. Your brother had become frail, and he knew it. The falls and the trips to the hospital told him he wasn't going to be able to live on his own without help." Her eyes sought to show sympathy, and the look was practiced, but not all the way sincere. She glanced back at her piles of folders.

"How did he manage to end up in the hospital?"

"With his heart, he was on strict orders *not* to take Viagra, if that's what you mean." Her lips tightened. She looked as though she were weighing the possibility of a lawsuit.

"But you have it around."

"For those with prescriptions, yes. It's not like the joke here. We don't give every male patient a Viagra each night to keep them from rolling out of bed."

Al considered whether he was supposed to laugh. He decided he wasn't.

"Will you be wanting to look at his room? You can't go through his things yet, since there's an ongoing investigation." Hope that she could be done with him had crept into her eyes. "I can have one of the orderlies let you in for a quick peek."

The first thing he noticed in Maury's room was the shells, hundreds of them. The door closed quietly behind him. Al stepped closer to the nearest shelf. Shelves lined each wall, even the ones in the small bathroom, and they were all covered in shells. He spotted a golden cowry he'd bought for Maury long ago, before...

He picked up a nautilus. The thing about shells like that one was they were made of chambers, one after the other, and the creature inside always knew which one to live in. He would have thought people would be half as

24

aware as that, but they weren't. He'd once gone out to rescue a little old lady from a snowstorm, and he'd found her in her kitchen, sitting on her stove. She was so tiny and frail he wondered how she'd gotten there. No ladder, and she was tiny enough to have needed one. The stove was not on—no power. In the other room, a fire was still crackling in the fireplace. He had no idea why she'd been in the cold kitchen.

Al didn't see many books, except for one shelf dedicated to an encyclopedic assortment, large and small, all on shells. He opened a side drawer in the nightstand, expecting porn. Instead, he found a leather address book. He was surprised Detective Fergie Jergens hadn't made off with it. Perhaps she'd just been playing the attempted-murder card to see if she could get a rise out of him. He slipped it into his pocket. She may have already checked the room, but an attempted murder still on a "maybe" status wouldn't merit a full crime scene investigation, by her or anyone else. He knew how that worked. It was always about money, time, and manpower. With over fifty thousand crimes a year in Austin, and fifteen percent of those violent, whatever had happened to Maury would get a lick and a promise.

Someone knocked on the door. Thinking it might be the orderly, Al went over and opened it.

A slender woman with black hair cut into a page boy stood in the hallway. She wore a tight black dress, and her dark brown eyes swam in a sadness and disappointment. "Oh. You're not Maurice."

"No, I'm not, and no one calls him that anymore."

"Well, I do." She leaned to her right, trying to look around him. It was a push since she was barely over five feet.

Looking down at her head, he couldn't see any grey

25

roots, but her hair had to be dyed. Her face, neck, and hands put her at about the same age as Maury, maybe even a couple of years beyond that. But she hadn't seen the hard wear that Maury must have experienced.

He stepped to the side so she could see inside the room, which was empty of any Maurys. He watched her eyes stop at the bedside drawer that he'd left open, then swing to him and slide down to his pocket.

"My name's Cindi, by the way, with an *i*. He tends to alphabetize by first names."

"Are you a close friend?"

She snorted, an unladylike huff through a nose that looked far too delicate and tiny for such a sound. "I was his closest... well, friend. But then, Maury... perhaps you'd best come down the hall and talk to me when you're done here."

She spun and walked with a gentle wiggle down the hall, the tiniest female hips Al had ever seen swaying beneath the snug dress.

Once her door had closed, he took out the address book. There were quite a few names, numbers, and addresses— almost all women. And as she'd said, they were organized by first names.

Five minutes later, he knocked on the fifth door on the left, the room she'd entered. She answered within seconds. Her face was bright and clean, and a bit of water formed a drip at the bottom of her left cheek. She'd apparently been washing her face.

"So you're the brother. He spoke of you, though you don't look like someone with a ramrod shoved up his tookus."

"Gee, thanks."

"Oh, come on inside." The wiggle of her hips was not as pronounced when she led him into the living room. "Is he okay? They don't let us out of here or I'd visit. It's like prison, a helluva place to wait on death, if you ask me. We only have each other for amusement." She waved him toward a sofa then eased into a wooden rocker covered by beige cushioned pads. The chair faced the blank dark face of the television. She had to turn her head to look at him. "Is he going to make it?"

Al hesitated. "I don't know. I didn't talk to a doctor. But he's still alive. I'm told he had a heart attack."

She nodded, started to say something, but gulped air instead. She closed her mouth, and a tear started down her left cheek. She pushed at it with an angry fist.

"Somebody said something about he may have taken three Viagras. Do you know anything about that?" Al was curious how she'd take that.

"There's no way in hell he'd ever do that to himself on purpose." She cocked her head, looking off at nothing on the far wall. She seemed to be reeling through the permutations of what Maury might or might not have done. "Nope." Her head swung back, eyes fixing on Al. "He wouldn't do that. No way. First of all, he didn't need to."

"Didn't...?"

"You know what I mean. Don't be coy." She looked as though she were suppressing a grin. "Maurice could have pole-vaulted through life when it came to being around women." She must have seen something in Al's face. "I'm not making you uncomfortable, am I? A little unreliable yourself that way?" The grin slipped out in spite of her efforts. She had wide, thin lips that knew how to smile in a suggestive way.

"You said earlier that you were...close to him. Was there something serious between you?"

"Oh, there was something between us, all right. And I thought we were serious. At least I did for quite a spell there. But you see, there's something wrong with Maurice, something that he fights but can't get the best of. He's... sort of an addict."

"Not drink or drugs. Not Maury."

"Of course not."

"Are you talking about sex? Women?"

"You sure you're his brother? You must've had a clue."

"So it didn't end well between you?"

"It didn't even end. I wanted it to, at first. I'm old-fashioned, believe in monogamy. But I came to realize that if I was going to have anything to do with Maurice, I had to share him. With many. Oh, so many."

"Do you have a key to his room?"

"Used to. But I gave it back."

"Does anyone else?"

"That I couldn't say, though I doubt he gave them out like prizes from Cracker Jacks. He wouldn't want any of the others walking in on him when he was... well, busy."

"You paint a pretty dark picture of him." He was far from surprised but wanted to keep her talking.

"Well, Maurice was a pretty dark man. But I loved him. At least, I'm pretty sure I thought I did." She paused then nodded. "Yeah, I did. Until he started to show his real self. I guess I still do, but I hated him too for a while. Maybe I still do some of that." Her eyes had gotten moist again.

Al hesitated to pick at the scab, but he had to ask. "What happened? I mean between you."

She sat up straight in the rocker. "At first he was everything anyone could have wanted, maybe too much. He had an intensity of passion that ran through me like a wildfire. I did and said things I wouldn't have believed of me. I felt like a teenager again, alive, full of everything that once made living so... worthwhile." Her eyes went blank for a few seconds, as if her mind were playing back

28

scenes she wasn't going to share. The corner of her mouth twitched up.

"And then?"

She nodded toward the address book outlined in the pocket of his khaki slacks. "Then I heard about someone else, and then another, and another." Her eyes welled up, and she rubbed at them in anger again. "They say when something seems too good to be true that you should depend on it not being true. Well, that was Maurice. He was the sweetest, best, and worst thing ever to come into my life."

"You knew he had a bad heart?"

She bowed her head. Then it snapped up, her eyes angry and dark. "I would *never* have done anything like that to Maurice, even if I knew where to lay my hands on those stupid blue pills. My heavens! If you knew how he was without them, you would have no more steered him that way than you'd put razors on a chain saw. For the good of the world, I wouldn't have done that."

"You know, I believe you." In her eyes, he saw a mix of adoration and hate and regret that could never have led to her hurting Maury. "But can you suppose that there were others who might want to do something that would stop Maury's... Maurice's heart?"

"Imagine it? I'm just surprised there wasn't a line forming to do it."

————◈————

Al checked the address again then turned his truck down the bricked drive that formed a loop past the front door. The house stood three stories tall, and the outside was of yellow stone irregularly shaped blocks, as was the paved path that led out to a garden, where a matching stone bridge arched over a koi pond. The vegetation crowded

29

close, thick and green, like that of a garden around a one-time showplace of a home that had been given the time and opportunity to overgrow while being cut back just enough to keep the paths open. It appeared to be a cool and comfortable jungle.

Through a gap, he could see the lake sprawling out behind the house. At first glance, he'd thought a million-five, but because of it being lakeside property, he upgraded his guess to something closer to two to three million. He rang the bell. No answer. He was about to reach for it again when he heard footsteps.

The door opened. Al felt his mouth drop open a half inch and willed it closed. Some women become more beautiful with each mature year, and the woman framed in the doorway was one of them, one of the best of them. She looked half his age, but he knew she had to have a year or two on him.

She nodded at him. "You must be Al. I'm Roma Hentchel. Come in."

The light was more subdued inside. She led him down a hallway, past a living room, and through a set of French doors. They ended up on a veranda beside a swimming pool. The area was enclosed and screened from the bright sun to form a cool oasis surrounded by the rich green of living plants. She waved him to some wrought iron chairs. A pitcher and two glasses stood on the round glass table.

He sat. "Lemonade?"

"Hardly." She perched on the chair opposite him and poured them each a glass. "My own recipe. Three parts of the best one-hundred-percent blue agave tequila, one part Grand Marnier, and one part Drambuie, along with the juices of a few limes and fewer lemons. I add a touch of confectioner's sugar to offset the citric acid. Don't say it's too early in the day. You're retired anyway, I hear."

He took a sip. The drink tasted tame and playful. But he'd been in that game before, where the Kool-Aid kicked into high gear, and the next he knew, he was swinging from chandeliers and doing a poor imitation of a rebel yell. "Just so long as you're not trying to seduce me."

"Oh, heaven forbid. Your brother pounded that out of my soul some time ago. I might try to get you to mow the lawn or weed the garden, but any hijinks are out of the question."

"I don't believe you have a lawn." He took another cautious sip. Still good.

"You're wondering about the flowers I sent to the hospital, right?"

He nodded.

"We were soul mates once. Well, still are. But that matters little in Maury's scheme of things."

"How so?"

"You may have noticed that I have money. Lots of it. I don't live too ostentatiously, but I live quite well. Maury could have been part of that—*was* part of it for a while. Then not."

"Did he violate the terms of the understanding?" In spite of himself, Al took another drink, a deeper one.

"I offered him everything. Everything. All I am or own. He stomped on, spit on, abused, disrespected, and otherwise made useless any idea of mutual trust and understanding." She cocked her head. "I hope I'm not being too harsh."

"Not at all. The consensus seems to be that Maury's idea of playfulness was not generally appreciated."

"There's something horribly wrong and sick with that man. He can't help himself, really, I guess. But it's an ailment. I don't know if it's treatable. If it was, I might have paid to have it done, though I doubt he'd have agreed

31

to that any quicker than being neutered. As it was, he was a Lothario, a Don Juan, a man on a mission, and one I could no longer abide. Has he always been like that?"

Al sighed. He looked off across the pool, through the green of the jungle. At the nearest pool screen panel, a mockingbird threw itself against the screen, trying to get inside to the lush paradise.

"He told me about what happened between you. I can see why you feel so betrayed." Her voice had gotten soft, caressing, and careful.

He turned back to her, pushing the rest of his drink away with his fingertips. His hand trembled.

When he didn't speak, she said, "If you're looking into this, you're going to find that there's an aura that follows that man. It's a cloud of betrayal. And you might just find someone willing to act on it. Me, I'm mostly over it. Mostly. But I've never dated again. Let me guess. Neither have you."

"Well, I am more careful about trust now."

"No. You aren't just careful about trust. I imagine you've given up on it altogether and set it aside, never to be used again."

CHAPTER FOUR

THE PHONE RANG.

Al's eyes snapped open. He blinked, looked toward the closed blinds, and saw no light behind them. Then he checked the clock—4 a.m. Cursing, he reached for the phone. He had long ago put an extension in his bedroom, but he should have taken it out once he'd retired. But it was the first call he'd gotten since retiring, except for the times he had been caught in here while making the bed.

An unconscious growl eased from his lungs as yanked the receiver from its holder. "Yes?"

"Didn't interrupt the hibernating bear, did I?"

"Who is this?"

"Fergie."

"And?"

"You'd better get down here. Someone's made another try at your brother."

He hung up and went to shower and shave. While his hair dried, he made a pot of coffee, letting it drip through a filter as he hand-poured hot water over the grounds until it was done. Then he fried two eggs in butter, cooked three bacon strips in the microwave—turkey to compensate for the butter—got out a bowl of cantaloupe chunks he'd cut from their rind yesterday, and put a few chunks on the plate. After pouring a cup of coffee and a glass of orange juice, he sat down at the table.

The light overhead turned the glass sliding doors that led out onto the porch into a mirror, a black one. His face was distorted in the glass, his expression pensive, unsure.

Whoever was trying to kill Maury wasn't very good at what they did. An amateur. Why did he care? He wondered if, deep down, he wished the person could be better at killing, at least good enough to succeed once. He pushed his plate away, food untouched, stood, and headed out to the car.

On the way to the hospital, he flipped through the news channels on the radio. He heard nothing about whatever Clayton might have been up to, and there hadn't been anything in the newspaper, either. Odd. But Al had his own issues to worry over at the moment.

He turned into the visitors' parking lot and glanced up at the scattering of lit windows of the five stories of hospital wall. The parking lot lights washed the brick surface white against the dark of the sky. Even at that hour, he could sense a low hum of activity inside. He wasn't in the mood to see or deal with other people. On the other hand, he could go home, dig a hole, climb in, and pull the dirt in on top of himself. Al sighed, pulled into one of the many empty parking slots, and climbed out of his pickup. His heels clicked across the hard pavement until he stepped inside and into the carpeted lobby. He flashed his former badge at the woman behind the reception desk then made his way to the elevator bank.

As the elevator door opened, Al was met by a uniformed policeman who led him down the hall to Maury's room. Al expected the cop to be lacking in cheer from the boring guard duty, but the cop neither smiled nor frowned—a robot doing a robot's job. The guy was probably okay with at least doing something indoors, instead of driving a cruiser and pulling over someone who'd been weaving across the center line.

As he entered the room, Al fixed on Maury. His brother's face looked even paler beneath its tan. Fergie stood on the far side of the bed. She held up a small clear evidence bag containing a hypodermic syringe.

She waved the bag a little. "Lucky the night nurse heard something and came bustling in. A big guy in a hooded sweatshirt was bent over Maury. He knocked the nurse to the floor getting out of the room, but it all happened before he was able to shoot whatever's in there into the IV drip line."

Al stepped around the bed and leaned forward to peer into the evidence bag. "You think there'll be fingerprints?"

"I think in a building like this, there must be about a million pairs of unused latex gloves lying around, some in almost every room. He's a fool if he didn't have a set on."

"The nurse didn't notice for sure?"

"She was on the floor. He knocked her down. Remember? First thing she did when she got to her feet was to check on Maury. Then she called security, who called us."

Al scanned the room. Nothing looked different, except the yellow roses in the vase had begun to droop. A couple of yellow petals had fallen to the table to rest beside a container of water and a plastic cup.

He turned back to stare at the bag. "Anything special about the syringe?"

"Nope. You could get one anywhere, even here."

He looked up at her. From where he stood, her eyes looked more violet than he recalled. Striking. Her hair was long and red, but he suspected if left alone it might be feathered with silver, though not quite as far along as his. Though he wasn't sure why, it pleased him she'd opted for long, red, and sassy, a far cry from her look in high school. He was starting to think a frown was her natural state these days.

She widened her eyes at him. "You aren't feeling a little frisky, are you? Trying to make a move on me?"

He backed up a step and felt the edge of the bed against the backs of his knees. Al hadn't dated or made anything close to a move on anyone in a long time, not since Abbie. He felt the low punch in the stomach thinking about her always gave him.

"Of course not." He said it a little too firmly, in what she might take as a defensive or unconvincing way.

Her mouth tightened into a thin line.

He cleared his throat. "I was just wondering why you aren't retired. You must have the years in for it."

"I have one or two things to finish up, then I'm as out of this job as you are from yours. Why?"

"Just curious." He shrugged. "When the brass ring of retirement came around for me, I lunged at it."

"Are you ever sorry? Find yourself sitting around on your hands, wondering what you might be doing?"

"No. I read, fish, and play chess." He didn't mention all the chess games were with himself. He was working his way through a book on Capablanca's best games.

"Any ideas about what to do with Maury here?" she asked.

"What do you mean?"

"He shouldn't stay here. Not if anyone can get at him. I'm pretty sure the department wouldn't go the expense of keeping a twenty-four-hour guard here. He's not a big enough deal for that. So what do you think?"

Al still stood close enough to look deep into those violet eyes. He was running through all the possibilities in his mind and didn't like the one he kept landing on. "What are you saying?"

"I'm saying"—she leaned closer and lowered her voice—"there's always your place."

"*My* place?"

"Yeah. Nice place out by the lake. Right on the shore. Got your own boat dock. Do you remember?"

"I know where I live. I just hadn't thought of taking Maury there."

"You mean because of whatever's between you?"

"Yeah. That."

"Well, he's out like a mackerel. How could he bother you?"

"I mean, he needs attention. How could I take care of him?"

"I could help with that."

He spun around. Bonnie, the curly-haired nurse, stood in the doorway. Light shining between the cracks of the closed vertical blinds painted bars across her face, making her seem to be peering eagerly out from a prison cell.

"I mean, if you could match half my salary here, I'd be glad to take time off and tend to Maury. It's what I do. I'd be happy for the lighter load for a spell, and I have time off coming anyway."

"There you go, Al. All your objections are taken care of," Fergie said. "So why the long face, Mr. Ed?"

A man with a long, lean face above a white shirt, red tie, and dark blue suit jacket over khaki slacks bustled into the room. "Hey, did I miss anything?" He carried two tall Starbucks cups. He held one out toward Fergie as he walked around the bed. He didn't even glance toward Maury.

Fergie took the coffee he held out to her. "You know my partner, Al. Walsh Turbin."

37

Yeah, Al knew him. Divorced. Three kids. Alimony and child support. Walsh seemed married to his job lately. Al would be the last one to have a bone to pick with that.

Walsh wiped the hand that had been holding Fergie's coffee on the side of his jacket then offered to shake. "Sorry to hear about all this." His handshake was firm but quick.

"Good news, Walsh," Fergie said. "We've got a safe place where we can move Maury. Out to Al's Shangri La on the shore."

Al held up his hand. "Hey, I haven't said yes yet."

Fergie tilted her head, and her long hair swept over one shoulder. Her mouth puckered up at one corner. "I don't really see how you can say no, Al. After all, he's your brother."

CHAPTER FIVE

A BLACK HEARSE WOVE THROUGH THE trees, eased down the last few feet of the drive, and stopped by the end of the sidewalk that led to Al's door. He looked up from where he was pouring piles of deer pellets for the small herd of fifteen, including three new fawns. At the sight of the black vehicle, the deer gathered closer around him and hurried to eat, while he felt the lump of lead in his stomach drop another foot deeper.

Fergie got out of the driver's side, Bonnie from the passenger door. Bonnie reached back to grab a small duffel bag. Al gave her points for packing light. She had switched out of her pink scrubs and wore blue jean shorts, sneakers, and a white blouse. Her hair seemed freshly washed, bouncing in curls, and her eyes sparkled. He felt the corner of his mouth twist. *Glad she's enjoying this.* For a moment, Fergie stood beside Bonnie, towering over her, reminding Al what a giraffe she was.

"Oh, aren't they cute." Bonnie chuckled and wiggled her fingers at the deer. "Is this your social circle out here?"

Al straightened. "Well, Spikey and Nora have been around since their mother brought them out of the woods to see me three years ago. They're twins."

Bonnie walked closer and pointed at a deer. "What happened to that one?"

"Three-legged Bob there is the biggest buck in the

group, but he's not been too pushy about it since the nighttime argument he lost with a pickup."

Bonnie looked as though she wanted to reach out and pet him but knew better. He would dart away, and then she would have made him do so hobbling on three legs.

Al shook his head. He didn't know why, but having anyone see him with the deer more than half embarrassed him. They might get the impression, however true, that the only friends he had were woodland critters, and he was buying their affection with food. He wanted to just shut up about them, but like anyone who spends too much time alone, he occasionally found himself talking on and on. It made him want to kick himself, yet he talked on anyway.

"When I first saw him after the accident, his leg was torn almost off at the knee. I didn't know whether to shoot him out of mercy or not, but he looked to still have a glitter of spunk in him. The wound got darker then black through the next few days, the damaged part of the leg hanging there, until one day it just dropped off. The stub healed, and fur grew over the wound. He gets around pretty good now, and he's acquired that 'it-is-what-it-is' look."

"But he's still the boss, three legs and all?" Bonnie asked.

"No. The bucks never are in charge. Nora seems to be the head matriarch these days. The others just keep showing up. I've tried to quit feeding them, but with the drought, I'm afraid they're not getting enough protein. I read that feeding corn to lactating deer isn't good for them, so I spring for a forty-pound bag of this food per week at fifteen bucks a pop."

"Well, aren't you a regular softie of an ex-lawman," Fergie said.

Bonnie dropped her duffel bag. "For my part, I think

Al's deer are really cute, and he's an absolute dear himself for taking care of them." She went around to the back of the hearse to help the driver wrestle out a wheeled gurney.

The deer had finished eating and were staring at Al's bucket. They moved away as Fergie came up to Al.

"Why'd you use the hearse?" he asked.

She grinned. "I knew a guy who owned one. Besides, it's less obvious leaving a hospital in that than in an ambulance with someone in it. Sorry if it gave you a chill of premonition."

Bonnie carried the IV drip bag while steering one end of the gurney that held Maury. The driver had the other end. Al and Fergie stepped out of the way.

"You need help with that?" Al asked.

"Nope. Do this sort of thing all the time," Bonnie huffed.

Maury seemed even more pale and withered than he had in the hospital. The bright light of the sun was less forgiving. They'd wrapped a trench coat loosely around his hospital gown, probably so he'd look less like a patient. He looked a lot more like a corpse.

"Did you have a hard time convincing the medical staff to let someone slip out from under their supervision when he's in this state?" Al asked.

Fergie's smile didn't make it all the way to her eyes, which stayed intense and focused on him. "They kicked a little until they thought about their responsibility if someone managed to get to him in there. Hospitals are all about risk management and limited liability these days."

"And you think he'll be safer here?"

She grinned for real, seeming to get some inner joy from his discomfort. "Well, he won't be less safe here with his caring brother to watch over him. Anyone who knows him probably knows about the rift between you two, so this isn't a likely place for him to be staying."

41

Al frowned. "I wish there was some other way."

"So you wouldn't have to deal with him, right?" One of her eyebrows arched.

He pressed his lips tightly together and looked away into the edge of woods that crowded close to his house. The thick green hid his place from the nearest houses on either side.

"Do you have a guest room?" Bonnie called from the porch.

"Yeah. Down the stairs. I'll help you with the gurney."

Fergie walked with him toward the porch. "You don't sound too enthusiastic, Al. You've lived alone how long now? Almost twenty years, isn't it?"

He looked at her. She was grinning like the kid who'd just dug a prize out of the pudding. "Why are you doing this? Twisting the knife. You've lived alone all this time, too, haven't you?"

"Most of it. Just since Reggie got shot."

"Sorry. I thought maybe there'd been someone new."

"Nope. He was a good cop, and a damned good partner. Not a bad husband, either. But that's been almost twenty years, too. I hardly think about it at all, except once, or twice, or maybe three times a day."

"Is Walsh a good partner?"

"There will never be another Reggie."

Al caught up to Bonnie and helped get the gurney through the door. Bonnie and the driver took the lower end while he took the upper, and they started down the stairs. He was surprised at how effortless they made the task. The gurney was lighter than Al expected, and Maury didn't seem to add much weight to it. They carefully eased the wheels from step to step until they were at the bottom.

The room downstairs had its own bathroom. That floor had a door to the outside at that level of the hill, nearer the lake. Instead of a storm door, he had installed a security door with bars. He hadn't thought about where Bonnie would sleep. There was a couch, or he supposed he could set up a cot.

He walked out to the end of the sidewalk, picked up Bonnie's bag, and headed for the house. As he went past Fergie, he said, "Come on inside. You can have a look around, get your bearings."

He dropped the bag inside the front door. Fergie followed him through the living room, where one entire wall was windows. He led her past the kitchen and through the sliding glass doors onto the upper-level back porch. From there, even more of the lake was visible. The breeze swept through to rustle the leaves of trees that crowded thickly on both sides. The monkey-like cackle of a pair of scissortail flycatchers up to their right in the canopy was muffled only slightly by the rush of the wind.

She looked around in all directions. "Nice out here."

The porch extended twelve feet out from the back of the house, enough to shelter the downstairs porch from sun and weather. He watched her take in the thick green wall of nature around them then the path that went down to the small boathouse and fishing dock.

She nodded toward the dock. "Most burglaries of homes like this happen from the water side."

"I know the stats. I haven't been hit so far. But that's why I added the security door downstairs."

"You may not have anything worth stealing, or maybe it's because you're usually home. But this time, it's not money whoever will come will be wanting."

"I know. You should probably take him back to the hospital."

"Nope, you're stuck with him now."

If it were up to him, they could have Maury. But it was a corner he'd already been painted into, so he shrugged.

She stared out across the water. "It's beautiful here, though. You have a lake view every day. It's a perfect place to retire." Not a boat was in sight at the moment, nor was there a cloud in the sky.

"You could always bunk in the boathouse and stand guard from there. There's a hammock down there."

She shook her head. When she turned to him, her eyes seemed to catch some of the sparkle from the water. Her long red hair lifted in the breeze. He was really starting to wonder if they were the same age after all. Out in the sunlight, she looked ten, even twenty years younger than he was. "Have you ever wondered where Maury's money came from?"

That brought him back to earth with a snap. "His what? I didn't know he had any money."

"I mean, how's he gotten by all these years? He used to fiddle with electronics, cameras, and, of course, his shells. But he hasn't worked for years. How's he get by? How's he manage to live in a rest home? They're not free. Far from it."

"I... I don't know. I just supposed Medicare or insurance."

"Oh, I doubt you've thought about it at all, as studiously as you've stayed away from him. But it is a riddle wrapped in an enigma."

"Hmm."

"That's all you've got? Hmm?" She frowned.

"Tell you the truth, I always thought it would be something like syphilis or gonorrhea that would take him down."

"That's probably how the smart money would have been betting."

"Let me ask you something, Fergie."

"Ask first, and then we'll see."

"Did he ever hit on you? Make a pass?"

"Of course he did. He's Maury."

"Is he really that bad?"

"Oh, he made it cute. He said, 'Take me to your ladder. I'll see your leader later.' It was vaudeville old but still made me laugh. I'm still laughing. But I said no."

"Did you say it hard?"

"Came close to breaking both his thumbs. I believe he caught on at last." She waited, but he didn't comment. "That doesn't bother you? Me hurting Maury?"

"I'm surprised he has any thumbs left at all, or anything else. He's been a very busy boy."

"He's no boy anymore. Neither are you for that matter. But you have less wear on the odometer, I'm guessing."

"Where do you think he got the money he needed to survive?"

"I don't know... for sure. I'd give worlds to know. I'm guessing it wasn't as a gigolo, though I wouldn't put that past him. There are still a few pieces missing to the puzzle."

The glass door slid open with a metallic rasp. Bonnie stuck her head out. She sniffed at the air, nodded, and smiled. "No salty spray?"

"We're not by the ocean," Al said. "When you can smell salt in this water, that's usually not a good thing."

She had a pert round face that also looked better out in the sun than in the pallor of the hospital. Her blouse was low cut, and she bent forward enough for him to see that her tan went as far as he could see. She held the pose a second or two longer than necessary in case he'd missed a blemish. "Wish we *were* by the ocean. But it's quite nice here. As good as an ocean beach to me. We've got Maury settled in, and the driver's ready to go. Mind if I settle in, too? I won't get into the single malt or anything."

45

"There isn't any good scotch, or cheap scotch, either. I don't keep anything to drink at home. I'm not saying I never did. I just don't now. Got out of the habit."

"Gonna make your retirement seem even longer, Al." Fergie took a last look at the lake. "I'd best go, or I'll miss my ride. Besides, it's starting to cloud up. I'll be back to check on everyone. Call if you need anything. Bonnie has my card."

She hesitated, giving Al a chance to look deep into her eyes, maybe to see what he was missing and would continue to miss, then turned and went inside to pass through the house. Bonnie held the door open for him, but when he didn't follow, she slid it closed behind them.

Al turned back, alone on the porch, to look out across the lake. He could take out the boat, but he was no longer in the mood. And he couldn't very well leave Bonnie alone. He wasn't sure what he was in the mood for, but the house behind him suddenly felt as full of people as it had ever been. Maybe that was a good thing. It just didn't feel good yet.

<hr/>

"You know"—Al looked up, and her small, round face was haloed by the light of the single candle—"I try as hard as I can. I work at it as much as I ever have anything."

"That's just it," Abbie said. Her eyes seemed huge as she held a bite of salad on the end of her raised fork. "You shouldn't have to work so hard. Keep it fun. Some men find it easy to do that."

"What kind of men are those?"

"Just eat your dinner."

He glanced down at the small tenderloin fillet, sweet potato fries she'd made from scratch, and the endive salad—all favorites of his. "You don't think Maury is a bit of a gadabout?"

"If by that, you mean he knows how to lighten up and have a good time, is that so bad?"

He remembered the giddiness of first being in love and the honeymoon feel of the early days, back when nothing else mattered. Lately, there were times he felt a tourniquet tighten around his heart. It seemed he constantly looked into a rearview mirror. "Who was that on the phone earlier?"

"Nobody."

"That was a long time to be talking to nobody."

"Come on, Al. Try not to be the clichéd suspicious husband. You're capable of so much more than that."

She put her dishes in the sink and bent to kiss him on the cheek before going to change clothes. He'd meant to shave before dinner, but she never seemed to mind the stubble. When she went out to meet her friend Susan, he cleaned up after the meal. He wondered. Hell, he was a detective. But he knew he needed to trust her. He could see her in every happy moment they'd ever had and even weathering some that weren't so... well, happy. Her wry smile, head tilted up at him, short auburn hair sliding to one side was his favorite look. Oh, hell. He'd surprise her for no reason, get her flowers, ask her where she wanted to go. Someplace nice. They needed to get away, to feel fresh.

The phone rang. It was Susan, asking to talk with Abbie.

"She's not with you?"

"No. Should she be?"

After he hung up, he went around the house, seeing it in a new light. Everything seemed familiar, yet quite different. He went outside, walked around the block then down to the park and back. Inside, he tried to sit down but felt restless in his favorite chair. He turned on the television then turned it back off.

He got into the car and drove all around town, out to all the favorite spots they'd shared. His throat tightened into a knot until he could barely breathe.

He drove to Maury's place, thinking maybe his brother would know what to do. Once there, Al sat in the car for a moment. He was being silly. He shouldn't bother Maury. There'd been times he'd even worried about Maury and Abbie, but he had talked himself out of that. No way Maury would sink that low.

As he reached for the key to just leave, the front door opened, and he heard laughter. His brother and his wife walked down the steps, clutching each other. They seemed so absorbed in each other that they didn't even notice Al's car parked on the street. They got into Maury's car and drove away.

Al felt unattached to the earth, as if he might float up and away. Emotions wrestled inside him—rage, self-pity, anguish, anger—hot, cold, hot, cold again. First, he blamed Maury, then Abbie, and after a much longer struggle, he blamed himself.

He squeezed the steering wheel as hard as he could with both hands. He knew what he wanted to do, what he really, really wanted to do. So he took several quick gulping breaths, started the car, and drove the hell away from there. If he'd stayed, he would have killed Maury. He knew that all the way to his still-shaking hands.

CHAPTER SIX

AL HEARD THE HEARSE DRIVE off, winding back down his lane. Its sound eventually faded, lost among the thick trees surrounding his place. He looked up and saw that Fergie had been right. The sky had started to turn into a grumbling grey headed toward black. *But would it rain? Of course, it wouldn't. Probably had forgotten how to rain.*

Al went inside. Almost every light on the upper floor had been turned on. He turned some of them off as he passed through the living room and headed to the kitchen, where he heard noises.

Bonnie closed the refrigerator door and turned around with her hands full. She went over to the carving block, where a loaf of German Jewish seeded rye sat. "How's Black Forest ham and Swiss on rye sound? Do you have mayo? I didn't find any mayo, just some funny French mustard."

He'd guessed from her little round belly that she missed few meals. On her, the waistline bulge was cute. It had been a long time since Al had anyone in his house. Each clatter and click of dishes rattled him like a subway train passing overhead.

"Yeah," he said. "That would be fine." *Take deep breaths. No reason to feel stifled just because someone is in your kitchen, digging through your fridge, and helping herself to anything she could find.*

"Why do you have a chess set in the living room with the pieces set up like someone's in the middle of a game? Do you have company a lot?"

"Never." He was sorry he'd said it as soon as it came out. He thought it made him sound like some stay-at-home nerd playing chess with himself. True enough, but he felt uncomfortable sharing that image.

Outside, the sky rumbled. A flash of white lit the entire wall of windows. The crack of thunder sounded half a second later.

Bonnie jumped an inch, a white ring around the blue of her eyes. "That's close. Isn't the count a second per—"

Crack! The lightning and thunder were simultaneous.

She dropped the butter knife beside the open jar of Dijon, spun, and leaped forward to wrap her arms tightly around Al. "A second per mile." She looked up at him then slowly pried her arms loose and stepped back. "Sorry."

The rain began to pound the roof, sweeping down in big slapping sheets. Had he been alone, he might have started a small fire in the fireplace, even warm as it was. To him, the rain made the sturdy house feel cozy. But with Bonnie's eyes still wide and her edging closer to him, he decided not to go for cozy.

He heard a motor coming toward the house—a boat's motor. *Who in the devil would be out on the lake in a storm like this?*

Bam. Bam. Bam.

Glass shattered and fell in the lower floor. He and Bonnie looked at each other then took off in a run for the basement. He beat her and raced down the carpeted steps, taking them two at a time.

At the bottom, he flipped on the lights. The glass from

two of the large downstairs windows that faced the lake lay in shards and pieces. The broken bits glittered on the tile floor. Only a mist whipped inside from the gusts of rain. The overhanging porch extended far enough to prevent the rain from pouring directly into the house.

Bonnie puffed down the last of the stairs and stopped to pant when she got to the bottom. She had seemed in better shape than that. He figured the panic from hearing gunfire was driving her gasping. *Well, hell, his heart was going a bit, too.* She held her knees with both hands and stared at the broken windows then looked toward the back wall. Al turned and saw three large holes high in a sweeping pattern across the wall. It had been a drive-by shooting from a boat. That was new.

Maury lay still and unmoved in the bed, which sat back far enough from the windows that none of the glass had fallen near him. Al went to the closet and took out some cardboard mailing containers. He planned on opening them flat and taping them up to cover the windowless holes.

"What's this mean?" Bonnie said.

"It means you're going to get to sleep upstairs, in my bed."

"Really? I think it means we should call 9-1-1."

"No." That came out a little too firm. "We'd just get someone like me out here from the sheriff's department, only with far less experience. I can do this, at least until morning."

"Are you sure?" Her voice quavered.

"Look, if I was the one called out here, the first thing I'd tell you is that the person who did the shooting is not likely to come back tonight. We can get through until morning. Okay?"

She nodded slowly but looked far from confident.

51

He nodded toward the cot she had set up. "I'll stay down here and keep a watch over Lon Chaney there. Is he in a coma or what, by the way?"

"No. Just sedated enough so we could move him easily and keep an eye on his heart until he's settled. It's a good thing he didn't hear those shots, though. My heart's still pounding away like Paul Revere on speed." She turned and started up the stairs, taking each step as if uncertain the next would be there.

He trailed along behind, not just because she appeared so shaken, but because he wanted to check the lock on the front door and those on the windows. That done, he followed her into his bedroom. She headed into the bathroom and closed the door. He heard her start a bath—not what he would have done, but maybe it calmed her.

What the hell? He looked up Fergie's number and dialed it.

"Hello?" She picked up on the second ring, sounding pretty awake.

"I wanted to talk to you about this idea of yours to stow Maury out here."

"What about it?"

"Someone just took some shots through the window from a boat."

"Did you call it in?"

"No."

"You're not going to call it in?"

"I think they're done for the night, and I didn't think we'd get any more help than what I could do myself. This investigation started with you. Do you really want the sheriff's department tangled up in it?"

She was silent for a few seconds. "No. Not for the moment. It's still our case. I'd like to keep it that way as long as the sheriff doesn't get in a do-dah about it."

"He doesn't have to know just yet."

She paused again. "Do you think you can hold the fort down until morning?"

"Yeah. Of course." He waited for it. He knew what Fergie might say, that he was showing stark hubris or arrogance. *Maybe she'd be right. But now it's also personal. Not just to protect Maury. This was his home, dammit.*

"Look, I never worked with you on a case before, but I hear you had the best record for closing investigations the sheriff's department ever had. Do everything your own way, but get it done."

"And?"

"Well, it seems like you have a choice. You have to find out the 'why' as well as 'who' is after Maury, chop chop, or you have to get him the hell out of there."

When he didn't respond right away, she said, "You kind of want this person to try again and to have to come through you when he does. Don't you?"

"That would sure put the cards on the table where I could see them for a change."

"And risk Maury?"

"Not if I do what I do right."

She surprised him by saying, "Okay then. I hope you're half as good as you think you are, at least the rest of tonight. We'll pop out first thing in the morning." She hung up.

Al got his 9mm Glock out of the drawer of the nightstand and slipped it inside his belt at the small of his back. He headed back down the stairs, where an evening breeze was pulsing in through the shattered windows. The air had a moist smell to it even as the rain eased up.

He took a few deep breaths then got a roll of duct tape from the closet and started taping the cardboard into place. Outside, the rain settled into a steady downpour.

The thunder sounded farther and farther away with each rumble. He kept his ears open, though he couldn't have heard a boat motor over the rain. That didn't keep him from staying awake and listening for quite a while into the night.

Bonnie woke to find herself naked, wet, and shivering in Al's big Jacuzzi bathtub. She hadn't turned on the jets. Just being immersed in the warm water had comforted her. Her head rested on the slope of the tub. The water was no longer warm. It was probably room temperature, but it felt far colder than that. She opened the drain, stood, grabbed a towel, and rubbed herself briskly to help her circulation warm her.

The house was quiet. After drying off, she went out into the bedroom and climbed into Al's bed. Under the sheet and bedspread, she warmed up quickly. The bed smelled of Al, in a good clean way. She liked the smell, the same way she liked confidence in a man. Even over-confidence could be an attractive thing, unless it got her killed.

She would have thought about that some more, but after she reached out and turned off the light, sleep swept over her almost immediately.

The next morning, Al led Fergie and Walsh Turbin down the steps.

"You know, this isn't our jurisdiction," Walsh said. "You should call the sheriff's office."

Fergie glanced back toward her partner. "He knows who to call, Walsh. He used to work for the sheriff."

Walsh was a big man, Fergie's height though more

blockish, and wide in the shoulders, with a long square jaw. He looked around the downstairs room, past the bed where Maury lay to the cardboard-covered windows, then to the holes in the wall where the bullets had gone. The holes were bigger.

Al pointed out the three chunks of lead on the low table beside the cot where he'd spent the night. "I dug them out. That's what you'd have done anyway. I know you can't drag your forensics team out here. They look like deer slugs from a shotgun. The shots sounded loud enough for that."

"Must've sounded like the last clap of doom coming at night and in a storm like that." Fergie moved close to pick up the spent slugs, weighed their heft in her hand, and then dropped them into the end of a small manila envelope she took out of a pocket.

"Those didn't come out of any pistol. That's for sure." Walsh peered through the window around the edge of one of the pieces of cardboard. "Had to come from the lake."

Al nodded. "Yeah, we heard the boat."

"Helluva time to be boating." Walsh turned to face Al. "Didn't wake Sleeping Beauty here, though."

"He was pretty heavily sedated to get him out here. And that still hasn't worn off."

"Walsh and I took a look around outside," Fergie said. "This may have seemed like the safest room when we brought him here, but I think we should move him upstairs for now. Those shot-out windows won't help the safety of the downstairs or the house in general."

Al shrugged. "I'll have them boarded up before I leave today."

Fergie frowned. "I'm okay with taking a personal day, staying out here while you keep after what's behind this. Walsh and I discussed it. But there may be a time when

55

we have to run some of this through the sheriff, just to keep him in the loop. You know how he is. Do you think he's going to bend your way?"

"Yeah," Al said. "He owes me one or two. Besides, he's working hard on something else that has nothing to do with this... I hope."

"I hope so, too. For your sake," Fergie said. "Bonnie, you'd best get down here."

Walsh went over to stand by the bed. "Well, let's get this over with. I've got to roll to get back to the city."

Since the gurney had been taken away in the hearse, they slid Maury onto a blanket. Al and Walsh took the shoulders, Bonnie and Fergie the legs. Bonnie carried the IV bag, though they'd started up the stairs before she could get ahead of them.

Al was calling out a cadence to keep them together, "One, two... step," when Maury began to twitch and move his arms.

When they were halfway up the stairs. Maury's eyes snapped open wide. He looked at Al, down at the women, then at Walsh. He bent at the waist and began to struggle. His first word was a rusty scream. "Nooo!"

Bonnie tried to give him a reassuring pat as well as hold him still. "Calm down, Maury. We're just helping you up the stairs."

He wasn't having any of it. Maury's legs twisted and kicked as much as his arms flailed. There was no real power to any of it, but he definitely made carrying him up the stairs more difficult. Bonnie squeezed in beside Maury and fought to steady the waving arm on that side so he wouldn't pull out the IV.

Maury began wailing. "No. No. No. I won't go. You can't take me there. Where am I? What do you want? Let me go! Go. Go. I want... you've got to... wait. Let me go. I want..."

Once in a plane, Al had sat beside a small boy riding with his grandmother. As the plane door closed, the boy became hysterical and had started kicking and thrashing. He screamed that he wanted off the plane, that he wouldn't go, that he wanted his Papaw, and that he was going to throw up. "Now! Now! Now!" But that demonic kid had nothing on Maury.

Al looked down at Maury's flushed red face. His brother's eyes were squeezed shut, and his head tossed from side to side. An onlooker might have thought they were the Aztecs taking him up to the altar to cut out his living heart instead of people trying to save him by moving him out of the path of previous gunfire.

Al grabbed the flailing arm. "Maury! Snap out of it. Calm down. We're just trying to help. What the hell's the matter with you?"

"Yelling won't help, Al," Bonnie said. "Think about it. He probably doesn't even remember being taken to the hospital."

"Why won't he calm down?"

"Give me a minute." Bonnie handed the IV bag to Fergie, who held one kicking leg, and squeezed past Al. A good part of her pressed against him in the process. Then she shot up the stairs.

They'd only made it up a few more steps, and Maury had managed to tear the end of the IV's tube out of his arm, when Bonnie scampered back down the stairs to them. She didn't appear as out of breath as when there had been gunshots involved. She held a syringe in one hand. As soon as she struggled past Al again, she took a firm hold of Maury's waving arm and jammed the needle in.

Maury slowed like a toy winding down. By the time

they hit the top step, Maury was out. The rest of the move went easier.

As they eased him into Al's bed, Bonnie gave a possessive look around. "This is a good room. I like it up here."

"We'll move your cot up here," Al said. He glanced around, already missing his room—the deep bath, the enclosed shower, the walk-in closet with all his clothes. He'd done all the work himself, and with very little real cost, though with lots of hours of hard labor. Al got great satisfaction from doing things himself. It stung him to give up his own bedroom in his sanctuary of a house. There were times in the past when he'd resented Maury, but that resentment was growing to a new level.

The others got Maury settled, and Bonnie set up the IV drip, while Al gathered a few things and prepared for his exile to a less cozy spot. Walsh eased out the bedroom door, seeming eager to leave. A minute later, Al heard him heading for the front door.

Fergie caught Al's expression and let out a soft chuckle. She seemed to be enjoying his angst a hell of a lot more than he was. She turned and walked out of the room as well.

"Yep, these are sure nice digs." Bonnie stood, stretched her back and rubbed her hips. "I'm guess I'll be all right on a cot up here, though I think I'd enjoy it even more if you were the one in here with me." She arched her eyebrows at him.

CHAPTER SEVEN

A L GLANCED AT THE ADDRESS in Maury's little black book and got out of his pickup. He walked up the front walkway and pressed the doorbell. The stained-glass front door swung open a second later. Al's jaw started to drop, and he snapped his mouth shut.

Angel Smith was petite with Asian features—dark eyes, shiny black hair, and the pale skin of a porcelain doll. Her grin held pure mischief waiting to spring at him. "Oh, I get that all the time. People see the name Smith, and they assume. I kinda catch 'em off guard. You're the brother— Al, right? I'm glad you called first. Come on in." She wore gym shorts, sneakers, and a tank top with a darker sports bra beneath that. A patina of sweat glistened on her tanned shoulders.

She turned and led the way to what may have once been a living room but now held a big screen television, an elliptical exercise bike, a treadmill, and a rack of blue, plastic-coated free weights. "I was married once. Didn't work. That's where the Smith comes from. It was cute, so I kept it. The husband, not so much. Though I did get the house. I was a good housekeeper, so I kept it. I don't know who said that first, but I claim it now."

The TV volume was set high, and what sounded like disco music accompanied a group of women in tights doing exercises that would have sent Al to an emergency room.

Angel stepped around a stand of plastic steps to grab the remote and flick off the television. Al sighed in relief.

She grabbed a towel off the treadmill's arm and rubbed at her neck. "Are you here about Maury? I'm not the one who gave him the heart attack, although we tried for that pretty good from time to time."

"You and Maury dated?"

"I wouldn't call it that. Surely you know about the others."

"I do but didn't know if I dare bring it up."

"Oh, I know all about the others. All of them. I think I was the only one he could talk freely with about all that."

"And you didn't mind?"

"No. The others maybe did. Not me. Maury used to call me, he said, when he was in the mood for Chinese. Our little joke. I'm not even Chinese. I'm Vietnamese. Well, second generation. Hey, I'm gonna have some Gatorade. Can I get you anything? Coffee? Vodka?"

She headed for the kitchen. He tried to keep his eyes off her swaying gym shorts as he followed, but she had the second tiniest butt he'd ever seen, at least that week.

"Just water." His voice came out as a near croak.

She pulled a tall glass from a cabinet and filled it with ice and water from the fridge door. After handing him his drink, she got out a green Gatorade and went out the kitchen door to a deck that overlooked a garden of ferns. She sat at a round wooden table beneath a sun umbrella. He took the seat across from her.

"Do you notice anything?" she asked.

He studied her round face, which was about the size and shape of Abbie's. His thoughts drifted for a moment.

She laughed. "Not me, silly. The garden."

He looked around. Below the deck, a path of red cinders wove through thick beds of ferns. Old oak trees formed a canopy over the backyard. Only small speckles of light made it down in beams to the yard. Around each bed of ferns a row of conch shells faced out, their pink insides like ears. The path led to a tiered fountain where water trickled down a series of slate steps to a pool. A bench with wrought iron sides and wooden slats across the seat and back stood beside the pool.

"Ah. The shells. Do you collect them too?"

"Hell no."

He frowned. "Did you get them from Maury?"

"Of course. Though why he kept getting them is beyond me. He didn't care much for conchs compared to all the other delicate specimens in his collection. But the darn things kept rolling in. Worthless, he said, except as garden decorations."

"Why so?"

"They're 'knocked,' every one of them. That's where someone's taken a screwdriver or the tip of another shell and knocked a hole in the small end so they can cut out the clasping end of the living conch and make that into chowder or conch fritters. It's a wonder any are left in the ocean. They toss the knocked shells into piles. No one wants them, not even the tourists, once they're knocked. Yet Maury kept getting them."

Al was enjoying the animated sparkle of her dark eyes more than the garden anyway, so he stayed fixed on her. "I suppose someone could make lamps out of them. But that's a damn-all lot of lamps. And if you're not in the lamp-making mood, I guess the garden's as good a place as any for them."

"Nice of him to share his worthless leftovers with me, don't you think? Shells. Did you read anything into that? Him collecting things of beauty? Yet I got these. I wondered what he gave the others but didn't fret over it much."

"You said you knew about…"

"All the others? Sure. I'm probably the only one of them who knew everything, or at least didn't have to figure it out on her own."

"You were okay with it?" He took a sip of his water. It was cold enough to numb his lips.

"It was Maury. I knew that about him from the first moment I met him."

"You didn't mind?"

She shrugged, a delicate gesture, one that hinted of the dignity of her Asian background and made him think of silks and fans. Her skin, which had dried in the outside air, seemed quite soft and smooth. She looked right at him, eyes black with intensity, and for a flicker of a second, he saw Abbie.

"Are you okay?" she asked.

He shook off the memory. "Fine. The others?"

"It was just as well. One person would have never been enough for Maury. Plus he needed the feel of conquests. He was Don Quixote, only it wasn't windmills at which he was tilting."

"Nor was it a lance."

"Oh, he had a lance all right, and he knew how to use it. I didn't mind. That's what you're after, isn't it? He scratched my libido, and I scratched his. I have a big one, but it was a mouse in the room next to his elephant."

"I always heard elephants fear mice."

"He respected me, or came to. I made sure of that. But it was different with us. We both got it right away about what kind of people we are and what we wanted. I didn't want marriage. I didn't want him here all the time. I quickly tire of the close proximity of people. In fact, if you don't have more questions, I'd like to get to the shower.

Unless..." Her dark eyes flicked to the house then returned to him, sparkling with a hungry glitter.

"I'd better get going. I... I have a lot to do."

———◆———

Al started for his house then changed his mind and turned his pickup toward the rest home, which was way on the other side of Austin. The midafternoon traffic was sparse. He could still make it home before rush hour if he really moved.

Gladys Willstone met him this time and even opened the door to Maury's room herself, perhaps to see what had put the sense of urgency into Al, given the way he moved. Down the hallway, Al could see Cindi with her head and shoulders outside her door. She watched them go inside.

Al crossed the room and went to the mini fridge tucked beneath the desk on the far wall. He opened the door. One shelf was filled with twelve-ounce plastic containers of GeriGade. Al had seen the stuff advertised on TV as the energy drink of the baby boomer set. The idea had made him sad, more so now that he knew his own brother drank the stuff. Maury apparently favored Cool Blue Raspberry.

He turned to Gladys. "I noticed these earlier. Didn't know what to make of them then. How do residents get groceries?"

"We have a grocer who delivers. Everything goes through the facility so we can keep track of what they order. Someone orders three chocolate cakes without a good story, and we, of course, put the skids on that."

He bent down close, could feel Gladys leaning to hover over his shoulder.

He had seen no container of latex gloves in the room and probably would have worried if he had. "Tissue, please?"

She stepped over to the nightstand and tugged a couple

63

of tissues from their cardboard box. When she handed them over, he wrapped the tissues around two containers from near the front and set the plastic bottles on the desk. She started to reach for one.

He blocked her hand. "Don't touch those."

Both had the new easy-open tops for people with arthritis so they didn't go crazy over childproofing that turned out to be senior-proof as well. He unscrewed the tops and looked closely at the foil seals of each. He put the tops back on then opened drawers until he found a box of gallon-sized Ziploc bags. Using the tissues, he dropped the bottles he'd selected into the bag and zipped it shut.

"What is it?" she asked.

"The tops to these two have the edge of the seal broken. Just enough pills could've been dropped in, then the seal pressed back in place. The glue is holding pretty well. I doubt if anyone would notice unless they were paying close attention. But these two have been compromised."

"They have a shelf life of a year if they haven't been opened." Gladys came close to peer at the bottles in the bag.

Al walked over to the trash can and looked inside. Empty.

She waved her hand. "Oh, we clean the rooms. Maintenance would have taken anything out of here. Why? What does this mean?"

"It means I think I found out how Maury got his dose of Viagra. I have friends at the lab. I'll run these over there. They can check for prints as well as contents."

"Well, I certainly hope you don't think it was one of the staff here who did it."

"I don't know what to think yet. I'll have to wait for lab results before I know anything."

CHAPTER EIGHT

RUSH HOUR HAD CRESTED TO its worst by the time Al got in his truck outside the lab and started home. Instead of taking the shortest path through bumper-to-bumper traffic, he looped back into the city and fought his way south through grid-locked streets and intersections. He swung into the parking lot along some grey wooden two-story townhouses that lined the edge of a municipal golf course. He pulled a paper towel from a roll he kept behind his seat and wiped his forehead. Well, there was an hour out of his life he'd never see again.

All the shade-hogs had parked their cars where the sun wouldn't turn the insides into a soup of fetid hot air, so he parked in an open sun-splashed slot and cracked the windows. Pinky's townhouse was on the end, and her bright yellow jeep was one of the few cars nestled in deep shade. He expected that since she rarely left the house.

He could smell hot tar as he walked across the parking lot. The coating and painted lines were recent, and heat from the afternoon sun bounced off the surface. His face and neck had a patina of sweat by the time he rang the ground-level fake-pearl-in-brass-setting doorbell of her townhouse.

Pinky answered the door, holding a half-eaten pimento-spread on white bread sandwich in one hand. A burly gal with a buzz cut, she wore grey sweats and scuffed sneakers. "Okay. Can do. Give me a... okay, in two days. One day? How much? Well... okay."

She spoke into the air at no one. Al was confused until he noticed the Bluetooth in her left ear.

"Bye." She reached up, touched the headset, and nodded at Al. "Come on in." She waved her sandwich toward the interior. "What the hell's up with the world? Everybody wants everything yesterday."

"Job security for you," he said as he followed her into a ground-floor office that looked out over the golf course.

"Big whoop." She huffed into the room, plopped into a Herman Miller chair and spun to face him.

He took a seat on a futon against the opposite wall. On either side of the window facing the green fairway outside stood a half dozen flat screen monitors set up in a curve around her power spot.

She started to take another bite of her sandwich, then stopped and put the sandwich down on a paper plate beside the nearest keyboard. "What is it this time? What's the department want?"

He looked around at all her high-tech toys then glanced outside. "It's not for the department. It's personal."

"That's right. You're retired. How's that going?"

"I'm here, aren't I? Wouldn't you think I'd have the boat out on the lake and be fishing if I could?"

"Okay. Okay. What brings you here? What personal business can you have that brings you to me?"

Al glanced at a picture of Pinky and her significant other, Boo, with their two adopted Thai children, Chang and Eng. Both parents described themselves as truck-driver-looking gals, and when Al had asked Pinky years ago who was the butch of them, she'd said, "We take turns." He'd eased away from that subject and never revisited it.

"Can you still hack into about any system?"

She tilted her head and frowned. "Sure I can. What've you got in mind?"

"I mean you're not just saying that? Because some of the places I have in mind have firewalls up the ying-yang."

"Aw, go on. You know I'd be in prison if I really let myself go. I have to think of the kids. Aside from a little edgy day trading and the work I do for you guys—well, the department—I stay away from temptation. Unless there's money in it. What do you have in mind? And how much are you prepared to pay?"

"I'll pay what I have to. The job's about my brother, Maury. I'd like you to nose around some departments, see if anyone's interested in him, keeping track, or watching him."

"Your brother? Oh, that's right. I forgot you had one. What kind of departments are we talking about here?"

"Well, the DEA, the Justice Department, and especially ICE."

Her mouth opened, closed, then her eyes grew wide. She stared at him while she reached out with her left hand, found her sandwich, and brought it to her mouth for a bite. She chewed slowly and her frown grew.

When she swallowed, she said, "Oh, just them? No worries. You want anything from Fort Knox while I'm at it?"

"Come on. For someone of your skills, how hard could it be?"

"I'm not saying it can't be done, Al, but this is one whopper of a hornet's nest you're asking me to poke. ICE is Homeland Security. I get on the wrong side of them, and I may never see Boo and the kids again."

"I said I'd pay."

"Oh, you'll pay." Her stare intensified. "What sort of key words might be tied to Maury?"

"Oh, any of the erectile dysfunction goodies—Viagra, Cialis, Levitra."

"Maury just too embarrassed to get a prescription?"

"We're talking thousands of units. Trafficking."

"You sure about this?"

"No. I'm not sure at all. I'm fishing. But I think I'm in the right pond, or near it."

"You know, I heard that a huge shipment of Viagra had been stolen and the police advised the public to be on the lookout for hardened criminals."

"Oh, knock it off, Pinky. I'm serious."

"I was afraid of that."

"Oh, and another word you might work in is shells."

"Shells?"

"Seashells."

"I'm not even gonna ask. Okay, I am. You think someone like ICE is sweating shells?"

"Look, can you do this or not?"

"How about this? How about I poke for any threads of Maury, the blue pills, the shells, and go through the slightly less risky local and state law enforcement data files, see how that works out? If that doesn't hit oil, I can probe a little deeper, though it's trickier. That good enough for you?"

"It'll have to be, for now."

———— ❖ ————

Al pulled his truck into his driveway and got out. The backdrop of sky above the lake was growing darker by the minute. The sun had slipped over the horizon some time ago, and he'd battled the tail end of the rush hour getting out of town and back out to the lake. He started for the door but spotted a deer's head sticking out from behind a mountain cedar. Spikey. Then Nora led the others, fawns and all, out to wait around him in a circle. He walked to the shed and got them some feed, all while putting up with their "Where have you been?" looks. While they ate, he held the empty bucket and stood looking at his house for a moment, then sighed and went inside.

Bonnie and Fergie sat at the kitchen table with piles of red, white, and blue poker chips in front of them.

Bonnie looked over her shoulder at him. "Good. You can join in, or at least deal."

"How's the patient?" he asked.

"Sedated again. He'll keep until morning."

"I'm all in," Fergie said. She pushed her pile of chips to the center of the table.

"Again?" A whine crept into Bonnie's voice. She looked up at Al. "You gotta be aggressive in this game, and she's a piranha." She tossed in her cards. "I fold."

Seeing Fergie suppress a grin, Al told her, "I appreciate you're helping watch the place while I ran errands. Hope your partner doesn't mind."

"You know partners, Al. I had to go to the gynecologist last week. So Walsh says, 'What for? To blow the dust out?'"

Bonnie laughed, her shoulders shaking.

"He's only eleven years younger than me." Fergie came close to grinning. "Wait'll his prostrate swells to the size of an eighteen-wheeler's tire."

Al nodded. "Happy times."

Bonnie got up from the table. "I'd better go check on Maury." As she went by Al, she reached up to pat him on the shoulder. "Sit down and play, if you like. But don't let her talk you into strip poker. You won't have as much as a sock in twenty minutes. Don't worry, though. Once I check on Maury, I'm gonna climb into the cot. It's been a long day."

As soon as she was out of sight, Fergie asked, "Have you found out anything useful yet?"

"Well, I'm no longer surprised Maury is worn down to a nub. I'm just surprised he isn't dead."

"Yeah, it does seem that whoever is trying to kill him might just wait until Maury goes out like a snuffed candle, which could be sooner than anyone thinks."

Al felt a soft punch low in his stomach at that thought. He may not have spoken to Maury in twenty years, but he hadn't prepared himself for Maury's death, either.

Fergie must have read something on his face that stifled whatever she was going to ask next. Her lips pressed tighter in that smooth, pale face that her long hair framed. He felt himself lean an inch closer.

Al put his hands on the back of the chair where Bonnie had been sitting. "What do you suppose makes Maury do what he does? I'm sure he'll be right back at it once he gets well enough to pop out of bed. He's been cutting a rather wide swath through life."

"I can't speak to his pathology, but I can tell you about my brother, Crandall. Do you remember him?"

Al nodded. A string bean of a fellow as tall as Fergie and a couple of years younger, Crandall had a small, fragile face that seemed a little too tiny for his lanky body, except the ears, which may well have lifted him off the ground a time or two in high wind.

"Crandall was a bit of an outcast, a nerd in school. But when he went to Vietnam as a marine, his letters home started to sparkle. You can't imagine the change in him. He was alive, fully alive for the first time ever any of us could recall. I wouldn't have thought being in a war could do that for a young man. But he came into himself."

Al had a few thoughts on that. Before he could express any of them, she was off and rolling again.

"The thing was, he had to come home. He re-upped then came home after that. It was the classic 'dog without a bone'—restless, snippy, and a little wild. He was still as skinny as he'd ever been. If he stuck out his tongue, he looked like a zipper. But he had a fire gnawing in his belly."

"Adrenalin junky?"

"That's what we think."

"I recall the... accident."

"That was no accident. Crandall had started to do foolish things, anything with risk. He whitewater kayaked, rock climbed without ropes, and even did some skydiving. At least he used a parachute. The day of his so-called accident he was running his Mustang on a road that paralleled the train track. He was right beside the train, racing it, gaining on it. At the next crossroad, he tried to shoot across the tracks in front of the train. He damn near made it."

"Yeah, I was in on the investigation. We didn't know he did it on purpose, though."

"Well, the family knew he did."

"All for thrills. You think that's what drives Maury?"

"That and an insatiable need for conquest."

"Conquest, eh?"

"It drives a lot of men. It's apparently a gnawing manly need."

"Not with me."

"Well then, someone may have to add you to her conquests."

"I don't see that happening, especially with Maury here like an albatross around my neck. He gets well enough..."

"You're stuck watching out for him until you figure out who's trying to kill him." Her violet eyes caught the light.

One of his knees felt ready to buckle. Al eased down

into the chair, picked up Bonnie's cards, glanced at them, and tossed them back onto the table. "What kind of person draws to an inside straight?"

"One with more hope than sense." Fergie gathered the chips and sorted them as she put them back into their leather box.

Al sat looking off into the corner of the room. He drummed his fingers on the table.

"How's it feel to be back in the investigation business, Al? I'll bet you didn't expect this when you retired from the department."

"No. You have me there."

"How'd you picture your life about now?"

"Coming in from fishing each day. Fiddling around. Reading. Listening to classical music on the radio."

"Then Maury happened. Any idea what he was into, what has someone so animated?"

"I just have a few loose strings at the moment. I'm quite a ways from weaving them into anything like rope. Maybe I shouldn't have retired. Then I could handle this officially."

"You could always get a P.I. ticket."

He shook his head. "I'll stick to a fishing license."

She tucked the last of the cards back into their box and closed the lid then leaned back in her chair. He found her penetrating eyes disquieting. Her stare made him squirm. She must be thunder in an interrogation room. Then her eyes warmed, and that made him even more uncomfortable.

"They say you retired because your partner got killed. Anything to that, Al?"

"Well, I wasn't anxious to break in a new one. I'd just gotten Barrett trained the way I liked."

"He was your partner for twelve years. It takes you that long to train one?"

"Barrett was a special sort—a real bulldog on a case but a head of adamant. He'd get an idea, and that was that. 'Keep an open mind,' I'd say. Just a waste of breath."

"What happened?"

"It went down pretty much the way they had it in the papers."

"Tell me. It'll do you good. You've got something bottled up in you that's making you twitchy."

Al sighed. "We were the third unit to pull in at the Stoker place. The uniforms were there, and the Rangers had a car on the way. A SWAT team had scrambled, but it was fifteen or twenty minutes away. We're detectives, not front line guys. Sheriff said to wait until we could determine if Mrs. Stoker, Mary Beth, was alive. She wasn't. But we couldn't know that then."

"Barrett didn't wait?"

Al looked down at his hands. "He was beside me one minute. Next thing I know, I see him by the house, sidling toward the front door. We wanted to yell at him, but we didn't want to give away his position. I don't know what he was thinking. Be the hero. Something like that. Watched too many action-adventure films."

"Those film guys are amazingly lucky."

"And bulletproof. Skid Stoker wasn't fooled. He slipped around behind Barrett and put the barrel of his shotgun up under Barrett's chin. We had this happen to a deputy before—Bill Thomas. The perp there finally let Bill go, but Bill was no good as a deputy after that. He'd jump at the shadow of a kitten. Worthless. Quit and tried to be night security at a mall, wasn't even up to that. It drained whatever soul was in him and left him a hollow shell."

73

"That's what you were thinking would happen to Barrett, weren't you?"

"Yeah. I was standing there, wondering if there'd be enough man left inside Barrett for him to ever function on the job again. Then Stoker pulled the trigger and sprayed the insides of Barrett's head all the way to the eaves."

"So you rushed Stoker and shot him."

"Come on. I let him drop Barrett, turn, and level the shotgun at me first."

"Then you emptied your clip into him."

Al shrugged. "Might've been excessive. Sherriff said so. But he understood. I was eligible, so I retired. Saved me probation and counseling."

"You'd do it the same way again, wouldn't you?"

"Wouldn't you? Someone sprays Walsh Turbin's insides all over the place, you'd do something, wouldn't you?"

"Sure." She reached across the table and put a hand on Al's wrist.

He didn't realize until he felt the warmth of her palm that both of his arms were quivering.

Without speaking he stood and they moved outside into the cooling air.

The full moon reflected in the ripples of the breeze-combed lake. Fergie leaned on her forearms on the rail, letting the wind sway her long hair.

Al bent closer until he was next to her. Evenings were his favorite times in the hot season, when the waves of mid-July heat lifted, and the wind coming across the lake swept the porch with a cooler breeze.

She turned her head, and he started to say something. But their faces were so close, he forgot what he wanted to ask. The next thing he knew, they were kissing. It was a long kiss, full of puppy eagerness, the abandonment of repressions, and a touch of sinfulness, just enough to make it even more interesting.

When their lips moved apart, he kept a hand on the side of her face. He couldn't see the color of her eyes, but they sparkled in a way that made his knees almost buckle.

"Well," she said, "I guess that makes up for never kissing on prom night."

CHAPTER NINE

ERGIE ROSE AND WALKED NAKED across the room. She moved with the grace of a panther. Al thought, *Look at those legs! They go on, and on, and on.* His second, more jolting thought was: *Oh, Lordy. I hope I'm not becoming another Maury.*

He lay in bed, listening to the shower turn on and watching the sun try to struggle past the edges of cardboard still covering the windows. The downstairs was one open room except for the bathroom and laundry room. The head of the bed nestled against the wall on the same side of the room as the fireplace. He'd meant to put a pool table in there, even though he hadn't played any pool in years. Still, it seemed a fine solitary pursuit for a man dawdling away his retirement. Then before he got around to it, Barrett had needed a place to stay while going through his divorce. Al sometimes pondered if Barrett's stupid bravery that had gotten him killed hadn't stemmed from some of the *Götterdämmerung* of his marriage.

He heard a phone ringing upstairs. It stopped. Bonnie must have picked it up since he figured Maury for still sleeping off being sedated.

Al's mind drifted back to Fergie—awfully fit for a woman of her years. Where gravity had been cruel to some, she had defied it in the gym, at the table, and in the active life she led. He pictured her naked in in the shower, soaping her long limbs. The sheet began to tent above him. He grinned and shook his head.

What was wrong with him? It wasn't like him to leap into anything casual and sudden. He was the opposite of that. But he'd known Fergie for years, perhaps thought of her before. He recalled every touch of her flesh, how his hand had lingered and lovingly explored. That was it. He cared for her, deeply. *Oh, crap!* Well, he hadn't wanted it or expected it. Instead of thinking how he might get out of it, he felt himself settling in, getting comfortable. He threw off the sheets and got out of bed.

Footsteps scampered down the carpeted stairs, and Bonnie burst into the room. She froze, her gaze homing in below his waist like a laser beam.

He looked down and grabbed a sheet to cover himself. "What?"

"Oh, my." She blinked. "Oh, my." She wore one of Al's robes, and it fell open, offering a glimpse of both tanned and untanned flesh.

"What is it, Bonnie?"

She tilted her head when the shower turned off. Looking around the room, she spotted the pile of Fergie's clothes. Al expected one more "Oh, my."

Instead, she pulled her robe closed. Blushing to her hairline beneath her tan, she stammered, "Call for you. Upstairs. Someone was murdered."

Al saw the cluster of law enforcement vehicles ahead and turned right, away from them. He wove through streets of carefully manicured lawns, landscaped drives, and houses with residents who closed heavy curtains at night. Tarrytown was the section of Austin where the so-called elite lived—professors from the college, people with some

77

money but not enough for the multimillion-dollar mansions that poked out of the peaks of hills around the greenbelts farther out in the city. It was the community where James Michener once lived, quietly pouring out words by the bucket. It was where neighbors took umbrage to Matthew McConaughey bouncing around naked and playing bongos with open windows in the wee hours. He ended up paying a fifty-dollar fine for disturbing the peace. Folks said if he'd lived in South Austin, instead of complaining, the neighbors would have come over to join in on the fun.

Tarrytown was spread across an inner corner of Austin like one of those stuffy doilies that acted as antimacassars on old cushiony chairs. Its dignity was fragile but often defended with zeal. When a congressional intern hit and killed a female jogger early one morning, some residents were more ruffled by the fact that it had happened in their neighborhood than by the driver going off without stopping. The intern had hidden her BMW and gotten her male companion of the evening to drive her to work, where she didn't mention the incident until the police came and questioned her.

Al sighed and turned back onto the street he needed. The number of vehicles had grown and now included Fergie's unmarked car. He'd wanted her to get there first since the city cops would be on point.

He got out of his car and started up the sidewalk to Angel Smith's house. A patrolman in uniform stopped him then went to check with those inside before he okayed Al to enter the house.

Fergie and Walsh stood on the far side of Angel's living room. The EMS crew was loading a body bag onto a gurney, and the coroner was putting his things back into his bag.

The sheriff, Al's former boss, Harold Clayton, stood beside the window, looking down at the floor. His shoulders were hunched like a grizzly rousted from a hibernation den long before spring. For a second, Al toyed with the notion that his former boss had been checking up on him, following his steps to see what he was up to.

"What brings you here?" Al asked.

Clayton lifted his jowly head in a way that heightened the image of him as a bear. "Woman called me. Said you'd been asking questions... about your brother Maury. She wanted to know if you were official. I said no. She said she had something she'd thought of that she was going to share with you. I said I'd come over, since I *am* official. You know I don't usually handle this sort of thing myself, but... well, it was about you, and there was the chance it was tied to some other crap going on. Thought it might be something I needed to keep close to the chest. You never know. She was dead when I got here. Looks like someone worked her over good then finished her off with one of her little blue dumbbells. Helluva thing to be killed by a dumbbell."

Al knew the sheriff was incapable of humor. He wasn't in much of a mood for a chuckle himself. Blood smeared the carpet where the body had been removed. He could see her pert body flowing gracefully through the room, fit of mind and alive. *That damned Maury.* Where he walked, the grass died beneath his steps.

"Well, we won't know what she wanted to share now," Fergie said.

Walsh slipped on a pair of latex gloves and began to poke around. Al moved close enough to Fergie to feel heat emanating from her body, making his blood percolate. He wanted very much to reach out and touch her face, but he couldn't exactly do that with the sheriff right there.

Al kicked himself mentally. What the hell was wrong with him? He hadn't felt or acted this way since he was a teenager. Yet he was thinking about taking care of Fergie, of worrying about her on the job, of caring. They'd somehow become linked, connected, and it felt like being blindsided by a truck, but in a good way.

Maybe something similar was behind Maury's actions. Another thing to think about.

His cell phone rang. He excused himself and slipped off to the kitchen to answer it.

"It's Pinky." Her voice sounded stressed, agitated. "You'd better get over here. Now!"

He started through the house, heading for the front door.

Clayton stepped into the path of Al's escape route. "Hold your horses there a minute, Al."

Al stopped, made himself relax, though he realized he'd slipped into a parade rest stance.

"I suspect you've been pretty busy with that brother of yours."

"Pretty busy. Yeah."

"You didn't call in a shooting at your place. You forget about that, or figure you'd handle it yourself?"

"I... I..."

Clayton put a hand on Al's shoulder. "Look, I'm not busting your chops. You were an asset to me for plenty of years there. I'm just trying to keep a handle on this in case any of it spills out to my turf." He nodded toward the blood smear on the carpet. "Just don't keep this to yourself. Reach out. Communicate. Okay?"

Al weighed everything behind Clayton's steely grey, unblinking eyes, the way he would a chess opponent. "You think that's what happened with Barrett? That I didn't communicate enough?"

"I don't think this has one damn thing to do with Barrett. You want back in the department, I'll take you

in a New York nanosecond. Just use the help you have...
while you can." He removed his hand and lumbered out
the door.

The spot on Al's shoulder still felt warm. He decided
it might be a good time to give Fergie Maury's little black
book. He dug it out of his pocket and headed toward her.

"The women in this book might be in danger now, too,"
he said, holding it out to her.

She arched one eyebrow at him and took the book.
When their hands touched, he blushed to the roots of his
hair, and she suppressed a giggle.

———————◄◆►———————

Al pulled into Pinky's lot and spotted a sliver of a parking
spot in the shade. He parked his truck, got out, and
headed for her townhouse. He knew why there'd been a
spot as soon as he neared the door.

Boo came out with two suitcases. She had the same
short-cropped hair and truck-driver build as Pinky. She
slid them into the back of her yellow jeep that had been
backed up to the front door. "There he is," she said to
Chang and Eng, who came out behind her.

They both carried shopping bags full of food. Each
wore a backpack and struggled with their loads, but they
grinned like two kids headed for Disney.

"Thanks ever so humping much," she said. Boo could
cuss a streak that would make longshoremen blush, but
she apparently toned it down for the kids. Al just assumed
it wasn't on his account.

Al saw the jeep was nearly full. Just enough room
remained for its four passengers. "What's up?"

The boys handed Boo their bags, and she stowed them
in the back. The kids clambered into the back seat and

strapped on their seat belts. Their grins stayed stretched in place across their eager faces.

Boo gestured at the house. "She's inside. You'd best talk, and quickly. Thanks to you, we've decided to take a vacation. Australia was mentioned, and New Zealand came up. But I have kin in Utah, and we're bustling in that direction unless you feel like forking over for plane tickets."

"I'd better have that chat with Pinky." He eased around Boo and her scowl.

He wanted to suggest that she might be the butch one, at least for that day. That thought held only until he was inside and saw Pinky's face. His steps slowed.

"Oh, yeah." She looked up at him from where she was sliding a laptop into a hard-shell case. "Just poke around ICE a little, and the DEA. No worries."

"Hey, I didn't want you to take any aberrant risks. You've told me many times you can hack into anything."

"I can. Only I don't usually get spotted."

"But this time you were?"

"Exactly."

"Is someone going to come after you?"

"I don't know. I just caught the spikes and thought, 'Pinky, it's time you put some ground between you and whoever these guys are.'"

"Spikes? Guys?"

"Yeah. I apparently kicked at least a couple of hornet nests."

"What was Maury into?"

Pinky closed the computer case and started to gather modems and wires. The thing about her job was that she could do it anywhere. She was about to become a mobile unit.

"Here's what I was able to find out so far. At least

the stuff that seems to have painted a big bull's-eye on Maury's stupid head. You were right. It had something to do with shells." She shoved a handful of wires into a cloth tote bag, shoved them hard.

"Well?"

"Some time ago, Maury registered as a marine biologist. He filled out the forms with Fish and Wildlife so he could import shells for study. Perhaps on purpose, he left the bodies in a few so the boxes would smell, maybe go through customs quicker. Thing is, you're not supposed to import dead animals. The boxes were searched. No drugs or anything. But ICE started a file on Maury, figured he'd made a test run and would soon try to import some of the fake drugs being manufactured around the world and slipped into America by quite a few people. A Jordanian fellow got nabbed. Another guy with Chinese roots went down. Not many Americans are dumb enough to think they can get away with it. Even Maury eventually backed off from that."

"That was it, then?"

"Not quite. That's when Maury started to get packages—first from San Diego, then from Key Largo. A lot of them got through. Those Homeland Security people may lumber, but they get there in the end. They figured out Maury had become part of a distribution network. There were a lot of saps like him involved. The pattern was for someone to set up the deliveries through a fall guy, someone who could be the first line if anything went wrong."

"And you think that's what happened to Maury?"

"Well, you have him getting by with no visible income and these boxes coming his way with worthless shells he throws out. Doesn't that give you a little whiff of limburger?"

"So it's just counterfeit drugs? Well, those wouldn't

have been enough to put him in the hospital if someone laced his drink."

"This isn't just fake stuff. There were a series of truck heists. 'Cargo theft,' it's called. Entire semis get boosted while the driver is at a roadside rest or in a greasy spoon along the road. Altogether, it amounts to major hauls, and the stuff is hitting the streets. They say the money gets sent overseas to fund terrorism. All kinds of agencies are trying to track down the threads of distribution. The FBI and ICE share a database called Cargonet. Maury's name is in it. Though Maury might've been only a tiny part of one of these, I've apparently pricked the balloon that may have these suit-and-tie goons coming to ask me questions I don't want to answer. So me and Boo are out of here in a raggedy cloud of dust. The kids think it's high adventure. I'm just hoping there's no thrilling chase scene along the way. How about I e-mail you an address where you can send a check once I find out where I am? Okay?"

"That'd be fine."

He followed her out the door and watched as she popped into the driver's seat. The jeep pulled away with a snapping, irritated chirp of tire rubber. The two kids waved at him through the back window as the yellow jeep shot out of sight. *Isn't life just like that—duller than stale toast one minute and like a basement full of lit fireworks the next?*

His phone rang. He pulled it out and answered on the way back to his truck.

"You'd better get out here," Bonnie huffed.

"Why?"

"Well, for one, your house is on fire."

"On fire?"

"Don't worry. I called the department before I scooted outta there and didn't look back."

"Where are you now?"

"Out on the lake in your boat. Had to drag your brother down the stairs and out to the boat like a wet bag of sand. So are you comin' out soon as you can?"

"I'm on my way."

He hopped into his truck and peeled out of the lot. Try as he might, he couldn't avoid thinking of the line in *Alice in Wonderland* in which Alice says, "Curiouser and curiouser."

CHAPTER TEN

AL PULLED INTO HIS DRIVE then had to ease off to one side. The guys from the volunteer fire department were just getting the last of their hose back into the red truck, and they waved at him. Wayon Gallard turned and started walking toward Al. There was no sign of the deer, not even three-legged Bob. Little wonder.

"Lucky I was nearby," Wayon said. "Clayton said he wanted us to keep an eye on your place when we could. I saw the smoke. It's dry enough that we're in a burn ban, even after that little bit of rain we had. I'd have had to check it out anyway. I got here in time to use up my extinguisher and slow it." He jerked a thumb at the firefighters. "These guys got here in time to save the house."

One corner of the house was blackened, the windows on that side had been knocked out, and the front door had been opened with fire axes. The house didn't *look* all the way saved.

"An accelerant was used. Gas, as near as we can tell so far. Kinda ironic, Al. Probably came from your boathouse or the lawn mower shed." Wayon had fifteen years in as a deputy and had managed to stay as lean as the day he'd been hired. He had a lean face too, and his hair was still dark with only feathers of silver at the temples. He rubbed a rough hand across his chin, which had enough of a five o'clock shadow going to make it crackle.

"Did anyone see who might have set it?" Al asked.

"Nope. I came over pretty quick, too. Not a car in sight. Perp must've hiked in and out again. You live out here in a woodsy place. Gives someone a lot of cover. I found a spot up on that hill yonder where the plants are matted down. It's in clear view of the house. Someone was up there waiting. Up this way." He waved for Al to follow him.

Wayon set a brisk pace up the slope through live oak trunks, stands of mountain cedar, and a couple of scrub mesquites. They came to a knoll where the grass had been pressed flat.

Al bent close to make sure it wasn't just something the deer had done when they hunkered down for the night. He turned and could see his place clearly from his vantage point. "I didn't expect to have so much company when I picked out this place."

"Clayton says your brother was staying out here with you. We looked in the house but didn't find any sign of him."

"He's out of the way, for the moment," Al said.

"You'd better look around yourself and make sure nothing's missing. We've got a handyman on the way with some boards to close up the place. We'll put on enough police tape to make it look like a Christmas present."

Al looked around at the surrounding wall of vegetation. "You figure whoever did this was trying to flush me out?"

"Yep, and they didn't just want to shake your hand. Probably sat up on that hill with a sniper scope. When we got here before anyone came out, the guy skedaddled. That brings up the question of who you've riled lately."

"Not me. Maury."

"What're you gonna do about it?"

"I'd best talk with him."

"You might as well know, Al, that I've put in to test for the detective spot you left open when you retired."

Al turned and took in Wayon's eager, expectant look. "You'd be good at it. You're persistent and meticulous. I wish you well." He watched a bit of air leave Wayon as he relaxed. Persistent was a nice way of saying overzealous, but he knew there was no sense in taking that tack with Wayon.

"Thanks. I was worried you might have someone else in mind."

"It's none of my business or decision, Wayon. Clayton runs the department. All that's behind me. I have enough on my plate at the moment."

"And it looks like you're on someone else's plate, too." Wayon nodded toward the new blackened adjustments that had been made to Al's house.

"You were right here handy, cruising the area, and I'm glad for that, or I might be looking at a pile of smoldering embers. How active is the sheriff in this? He seems pretty involved."

"Well, you know Clayton. He's always been hypersensitive about anything anyone past or present might do that could reflect badly on the department."

"And he's got worries that way about me?"

"Oh, let's just say he's being his usual vigilant self."

The sun passed behind a cloud, and the area all around Al's house was cast into eerie, sinister shadows. He was far from being a superstitious man, but that didn't keep a chill from rippling through him.

CHAPTER ELEVEN

"**F**OCUS. FOCUS." AL SAID IT out loud, though he was alone in the truck. He drove fast, clenching the wheel. He barely slowed before accelerating the truck through each turn and tight curve.

First, he needed to get Bonnie and Maury and find a place for them to hole up. Next, he had to warn Cindi and Roma and any of the others in Maury's harem. All urgent. He tried to line up the algorithm of what he needed to do first, but instead, he found himself thinking about Fergie again. *Dammit.* Every touch of her skin had been a jolt, a shot back to teenaged exuberance giving him a sense that he was more alive than ever. He hadn't wanted that, nor had he been able to resist it.

Worse, he'd made himself vulnerable, and her through him. Everything connected to Maury was at risk—his house, already hit twice, and the people near him, especially Fergie. He'd forgotten how befuddled emotions had made him as a teenager, or when he had been around Abbie. He'd have to think more clearly if he was to operate in a world crashing down on all sides of him. Still, he could call her. That might calm him, help him think.

He pulled out his cell, screeched around a curve, then straightened the wheel. Before he could dial, the phone rang in his hand. He answered.

"Hurry, Al," Bonnie sounded out of breath.

"What's up?"

"It's Maury. He's come to. He's like an octopus on steroids out here, and there's no place for me to escape on the boat. I can't sedate him."

"What's the matter? Doesn't he realize you're trying to help him?"

"I tried the voice of reason. No go. I've seen a lot of different ways people come out of what he's been through. Some revert a bit until they stabilize. Was he a letch as a kid?"

"Pretty much."

"Well, it's a 'me, me, me' world for Maury right now again, and all paws at that."

"Push him overboard if need be. I'm about to the marina."

"Okay. I'm bringing the boat in."

In the background, Maury said, "If you're not doing anything with those breasts you should let me—"

Swack. He heard the hard slap. *Good for her.* Al hung up before he could hear Maury whine about the world being neither kind nor fair.

People who had never been to Texas pictured it as flat. But parts of the Texas Hill Country surrounding Lake Travis had valleys that looked like gaping mouths ready to swallow anyone or anything, including vehicles. Al drove through the valley that led down to the lake as fast as he could go. When he pulled into the marina parking lot, he could make out his boat moving in herky-jerk fashion as Bonnie sought to steer and at the same time fend off madman Maury. *What a jerk!* Al was starting to hope she really would just shove his brother overboard. As quickly that notion battled with Maury being his brother. Like it or not, it was the way things were.

Al climbed out of his truck and went out onto the dock.

The boat wobbled up, and as it neared, he could see that Maury's wrists were tied together with the boat's tender and lashed to a cleat at the bow. Good. Bonnie had taken matters into her own hands.

"You're gonna have to grab the bow." Bonnie shut off the engine and let the boat drift in to gently bump against the rubber padding on the side of the dock. "Tender's in use for something else."

"Good for you," Al said. He caught hold of the port gunwale.

"He's ambitious but weak enough to handle," Bonnie said.

Maury tugged at the ropes that bound him. "You see how I'm treated? A sick man and tied up like livestock." His hands weren't turning red, so Al let him stay tied.

"Just be glad she didn't brand you, the way you acted. What's wrong with you?"

Bonnie huffed. "Listen to you two. First time you've talked, and this is the best you've got?" She dug in a compartment behind her seat and came up with a spare anchor rope.

"No!" Maury yelled when he saw the white coil of rope in her hand.

"It's to hold the boat to the dock, you perv. But I'll save a length if you try anything else." She tossed the coil to Al.

Al made the boat fast, getting more of a kick out of Maury's squirming and pitiful moaning than he should. Just seeing his brother made Al want to wring Maury's scrawny neck like a chicken's. But at the same time, he wrestled with their history, the years they'd spent together, leaning on each other. Then he thought of Abbie. Maybe brothers on opposite sides in the Civil War had such conflicting thoughts, feeling the tug of brotherly love—right before they pulled the trigger. He stood up and looked down at Maury.

"Help me. Untie me." Maury's whimpering stirred more anger than pity.

"Listen to me. I want to know something, and you've got to tell me."

Maury scowled. "The first time we speak to each other in years, and you can only browbeat me. Don't let me stay tied up like this. I just got out of the hospital."

"I'm trying real hard to care, Maury. Now, tell me. Who were you working with here when you were getting boxes of worthless shells shipped to you?"

"No one."

"Don't be a fool. You have a partner. Someone was playing you for a dunce. This was a Dynamite Dave situation all over again. You thought your part was harmless enough, and you made enough money to get by. But all that's about as healthy now as your heart. So give it up. Who was it?"

"No. I won't tell you. You can't make me."

Al tilted his head. Well, that was his own fault. He'd let being irritated with Maury coming back into his life get to him, his causing Al to leave his home. Any other time, he would have used his years of interrogation experience to bond a little first and build up with less threatening questions. He'd given Maury a reason to sound petulant. He hadn't heard Maury speak in that tone since he was a small boy. Whatever chord that hit took Al all the way back to their childhood. How could he feed deer and care for others and not feel something for someone he'd known as long as he'd been alive?

Al bent down on one knee until his head was close to Maury's. The sun blazed down on them. He could see the light of it reflecting back from the water making Maury's ears translucent, the veins showing through, the nearly clear flesh as delicate as some of his most intricate shells.

"Listen to me, Maury. We're in real danger. *You're* in danger. Whoever's behind this is not messing around. You and everyone who knows anything's about to be blown away."

"You're just making this—"

Al held up a hand. "I don't have time to argue. I've got a lot to do and very little time. Your seemingly harmless way of getting by has touched everyone in a very bad way. They've already killed Angel—tortured her and brutally beat her to death."

"Angel? No, not Angel."

"She's in the morgue right now. Whoever tortured her got some scraps of information. Shortly after her death, someone staked out my house, set fire to it, and probably sat up in the woods with a scoped rifle waiting for me, or more likely you, to come out. Then that would have been it. *Bang!*"

Maury flinched.

"Now, will you tell me?"

"No." Maury lowered his head then raised it defiantly and looked Al in the eyes. "I can't. Don't you understand?"

"Hard for me to imagine how things could get much worse than this." Al shook his head. There was this, though. Now they were at least acting like two adults and talking. He tried to feel good about that, for just a second. But there was too much to do. He pushed off the wooden boards of the dock to stand and look down at Maury.

Bonnie dropped back into the seat behind the wheel, her chest bouncing pleasantly, though Maury's attention was still on his own tied wrists. "What now?"

"I'm going to have my boat dry-docked here. If you can watch Maury for a few minutes more, I'll arrange things."

93

Maury pulled at the rope again. "Hey, doesn't anyone care about me? I want to talk... about other things. Catch up. We can do that."

"There'll be plenty of time for that, Maury." Al spun and headed for the marina office.

On his way back from the office twenty minutes later, Al walked along the rows of docked boats in the covered marina slips. He heard his brother muttering before he was even close enough to see his boat. Maury's voice had shifted to a weaker tone, hoping perhaps to gain sympathy, though he'd been frisky enough a few moments ago. It was having as much effect on Bonnie as a light rain shower on an igneous rock. Not one to miss an opportunity, she had leaned back in the driver's seat and undone the top few buttons of her blouse to catch some rays. He could give the girl that much—she knew how to make a party happen wherever she was. No half-empty glass for her.

"Bonnie?" Al said.

Her eyes popped open, and she sat up.

"We have a new home, and it's just a short walk from here. But I want to tie up the boat to it, so I'll take us there." He climbed aboard and put his paper grocery bag in the shadow beneath the console.

Bonnie slid over to the passenger's seat, buttoning up her blouse as she did.

"What about me?" Maury asked.

"You'll be fine. A little spray of water will be good for you." Al turned the key and the motor roared to life. He checked the gauge—still half a tank. Good.

Al eased the boat along the No-Wake zone until they passed the end of the marina and came to a stretch where three houseboats were tied front and back, parallel to the shore. Each had a gangplank that led to shore. The one on the far end had a burgundy stripe all the way around its hull. Al slid the boat close to the back end of it, and Bonnie hopped out. She ran the rope around the cleats until she had the boat tied fast.

Al handed the bag to Bonnie. "You'd best stow these. I had to pay resort prices, so I got just enough to get by until I can swing by a regular grocery on the way back."

"You're going somewhere?"

"Not for long," he told her. "I've got a couple of people to visit, and I want to swing by my house to make sure it's okay. I'll get your medical bag, too, in case we need it."

She glanced toward Maury, who was wrestling gently with the ropes that held his wrists while trying, though not succeeding, to show no impatience. His facial expressions flickered between that of someone his age and someone far, far younger.

Al untied Maury, stepped onto the deck, and held out a hand. Maury took it, and Al hauled him up out of the boat. Maury felt much lighter than Al expected. Once standing on the deck, Maury rubbed at his wrists and glared at Al.

"If you're trying to assert your status as big brother, forget it. Right now, your stock's as low as your health. Now, get inside." Al put his hand on Maury's back and gently urged him toward the open sliding door.

As Maury walked past, Al studied him. His brother had lived harder and aged faster, but it was the same brother he'd always had, for good or bad. Maury didn't look as if he could take the best of three falls in a brawl with a kitten, but his demeanor was all strut and cockiness. Al couldn't help but briefly wonder how his brother managed that.

Al took a short walk to cool off and used the time to bring his truck closer. He sat in it for a moment or two before heading into the houseboat.

Bonnie was putting cold cuts and sliced cheese into the

boat's small fridge. The loaf of whole-wheat bread lay on the counter—the best of the marina shop's bleak pickings. She pulled out the little jars of mustard and mayonnaise and grinned at Al.

Maury had eased into the one easy chair in the room. It sat across from the dinette.

"There are two full-sized berths on this deck and a stateroom below," Al said.

"I call the stateroom," Maury said.

Bonnie and Al exchanged a glance. Al shrugged, deciding he would check to see if they could lock it to keep Maury down there. She reached into the bag and took out a six-pack of Heineken, which she popped into the fridge. She started to fold the brown grocery bag.

"Can you believe? Store was out of bottled water. Truck will come later today. So—"

Before Al could finish, Maury jumped out of his chair and crossed the room in a flash. He opened the fridge door, grabbed one of the Heinekens, pulled it loose from the pack, popped it open, and tilted it to his mouth. His head tilted back and Al watched Maury's Adam's apple bob as he swallowed until the can was half-empty.

Maury lowered the beer and grinned. "Ah."

Al felt the heat of anger sweep all the way to his face. He shot across the room, grabbed the can from Maury's hand, and rushed to the glass doors. He slid them open, crushing the can as he went and sending a cold wash of beer bubbling over his hand and wrist. He threw the can out into the water as far as he could then slammed the glass closed. Without a word he went across, pulled a paper towel from the roll above the sink, then turned to glare at Maury while he wiped off his hand. "What in the hell is wrong with you?"

Maury's eyes opened wide. "With *me*?"

"Are you an alcoholic now, too?"

"I was just thirsty. I've been through a lot."

"You're going to be through a lot more before this is over with. Hasn't it gotten through to you that this is as serious as sheet-metal origami?"

"Just thirsty," Maury mumbled.

Bonnie's head moved back and forth as if she were taking in a ping-pong match as she watched them.

"Look," Al said. "Let me repeat the high points. Someone's made three tries to kill you. *You.* They did kill Angel. Tortured her, found out from her about me and where I lived. Then they set fire to my house. Now, will you tell me who you were working with here?"

Maury shook his head without meeting Al's eyes. "No, I can't."

"You won't."

"Take it however you like."

"You were the patsy in what I can only describe as a sucker's game, and now you're just a tiny piece of a mess that someone thinks needs to be cleaned up. Wiped out. Whoever is after you, they're probably as dangerous as it gets. You don't even have the decency to go down alone. You're willing to take me, Bonnie, and any number of other people down with you. Now, will you talk?"

"No."

Al turned to Bonnie. "You should have just drowned him when you had the chance."

Maury sulked back to the chair and lowered himself into it. "That's all right. Just talk about me like I'm not here. Like I don't matter." He looked up at Al with those eyes that knew far more detail of Al's past than any other living person. Maury was defiant and had gone as far as he would go. Al knew that. Maury didn't get his back up often, but when he did, it went all the way up.

Al forced himself to take a couple of deep breaths. The rift between them had been about betrayal. Hell, Abbie had been as much at fault as Maury. What did that make Al if he insisted Maury betray someone else? *Damn.* He would to have to back away, not press, if he was going to be able to stand being around Maury... and himself.

Al turned to Bonnie. "I don't know how much time we have here. Not much, I'm sure. Then we'll have to be on the move. There are a lot of places on the lake where we can move around. I'll round up enough supplies for that on my way back. First, I need to warn a few of the people Maury has endangered."

Maury looked out the glass doors toward the lake, suddenly interested in the nothing going on out there. He clenched and unclenched his jaw. "You're the one who doesn't get it. I just can't tell."

"Maury, look at me."

He did, staring at Al while a whole gamut of emotions flickered across his face: mischief, anger, fear, then resentment.

"Will you swear on our mother's grave that you'll leave Bonnie alone while I'm gone? Stay away from her and the provisions unless she feeds you. Understood?"

Maury hesitated, the glitter of deception in his eyes. "Okay."

"You swear?"

"Yes. Dammit. Yes. I swear."

Al studied him, shook his head, and held up a finger. "I'll be right back."

He crossed the gangplank and went to his truck. He rummaged in the glove box, grabbed his Taser, and headed back.

Inside, he went over to Bonnie and held the Taser out

for her. "It's charged and ready to go. If he so much as takes a step toward you, then you light him up like a pinball machine. You have my permission."

"But that might well kill him."

"That's a chance he'll have to take."

CHAPTER TWELVE

AL DROVE PAST THE DRIVE that led back to his place and, a little farther down the road, slid his truck into an empty lot as covered in thick brush as his. Fishermen sometimes pulled in there to sit on the bank and fish, even though the land was posted. It was also probably where whoever had set fire to his place and waited to snipe at him had parked. He only had a short hike to his place, but the entire way was through the woods.

At first, he saw none of the deer. He would set out some food for them later, but they'd have to be on their own for a few days, a helluva thing in the drought. It was over a hundred degrees in the shade, and his shirt was soaked through before he'd gone very far.

At last, he spotted the brown of a deer. He moved closer. It didn't move. Normally, they were skittish and would leap to their feet and scamper away if disturbed. He walked nearer and saw flies. His stomach dropped to his ankles. He broke into a jog.

He found three-legged Bob lying on his side and knelt beside him. The deer's throat had been slit, and blood had pooled then oozed into the parched soil. Where the crimson fluid had dried enough, the edges were black. The deer still wore the resigned "it is what it is" expression, but the peace on his face hinted that he had died imagining himself running on four legs again.

The other deer had probably scattered, but Bob had been slower, and someone had grabbed him. *But who? And to what end? What kind of people were these who were coming after Maury?*

The sad lump in Al's stomach began to burn, and he realized it was becoming anger. He'd only lost his temper that one time on the job, but whoever had killed Bob had touched that nerve again. He struggled to get the best of it, forcing himself back to calm and to just feeling incredibly sad.

He rose slowly on unsteady legs and looked around. Normally, he liked walking through woods, any woods, especially these woods. But the area had taken on sinister shadows in spite of the glaring sun that pressed down on the canopy of live oak leaves overhead. He took a few deep breaths then picked up the pace as he headed for his house.

Once there, he hung back and watched, scouting all the places where anyone might be waiting. After a few minutes, he figured it was just too damned hot for a stakeout or bushwhack. He eased around to the front and saw that the handyman had done a good enough job so that no one was going to get in that way for a while. The front door and windows were boarded over and hadn't been disturbed. As Wayon had promised, yellow police tape crisscrossed the scorched area, and it was all still in place.

Al went back around to the rear, got out his keys, and slipped inside, feeling something like a thief breaking into his own house. He had little trouble rounding up Bonnie's things. Her small medical kit fit inside her bag, along with the few clothes she'd brought. Maury had come with nothing but what he still wore.

The first thing Al gathered of his own was his 9mm Glock. He slid a hand under his mattress and came out with the loaded Sig Sauer that took the same ammo. Fergie may have suspected that they'd been doing their horizontal mambo right above a loaded weapon, but that wouldn't have mattered much to a lifer cop like her. He put the two guns, a box of ammo, and extra clips for both in a duffel bag.

He paused in his packing and caught himself staring off at nothing. He had to sort out what was going on with Maury. But that didn't bug him as much as what had happened to Three-legged Bob. That just wasn't right. He knew it wasn't, caring more for the death of a deer than his brother. But he'd been around Bob for the past three years, and Maury was only freshly back into the picture. He shuddered, shook it off, and finished putting shirts, underwear, spare jeans, and sneakers into his bag.

He drove his truck down Roma's bricked drive, expecting *déjà vu* all over again as he stopped in the loop by the front door. Only something was different. From around the three-story yellow stone house, guys in black with masks, carrying assault rifles, stepped out from behind bushes and surrounded his truck. He counted four on the ground and could see another up on the second-story porch. That one was crouched over a weapon big enough to need a tripod.

Al rolled down his window and ever so slowly took out his driver's license. One of the men, who was already speaking into a small mic that extended alongside his cheek, took the license and stepped back. After a moment, he gave the license back and signaled for Al to turn off his engine and get out of the truck. The man held out his gloved hand.

Al dropped his keys on the man's palm. "Park it

somewhere in the shade, and there's an extra dollar in it for you."

Someone behind him jabbed the butt of a rifle firmly into Al's kidney, pushing him toward the house. They prodded him inside and all the way through the French doors, out onto the veranda by the pool. Roma sat in one of the wrought iron chairs at the round glass-topped table. She waved him to a seat across from her. He sat slowly, his kidney still throbbing, and took in the silver coffee service with delicate bone china cups and saucers. She poured him some coffee.

He took the cup and saucer she slid over to him. "No margaritas today?"

"Not feeling too jovial or party-like today. You?"

"Who are the men in black?"

"Former Israeli commandos, I'm told, supposed to eat Navy SEALs for breakfast. At least that's what the agency said. They're not supposed to kill anyone... unless they need to."

"Nice."

"Well, hell, Al. Look at the spot your brother has put me into."

"I'm afraid we're all in it. Not all of us can beef up the security to a DEFCON 1 level like you."

"That poor Angel Smith. The police told me about her, the brutal way she was killed."

"You weren't just inspired to take a trip to the far side of the planet?"

"You don't run if these people are as serious as I suspect they are. Of the flee or fight choices, I decided to spend a bit and stay hunkered down. How about you... and Maury?"

"I guess we're more on the flee plan right now. I just wanted to stop by and warn you." He took a sip of his coffee—pure black silk, would probably run about ten dollars a cup at Starbucks. He took another sip and decided to raise his estimate to twenty.

"When you see Maury, would you do me a favor?"

"Sure. Punch him?"

"No. Tell him I forgive him. He is a rascal, but in his better moments he could charm the socks off a snake. I loved that little scamp."

"You used the past tense. You don't think he'll make it?"

"If I was betting, I wouldn't even have him to place or show."

In his escorted walk back to his truck, during which he kept his mouth tightly zipped, he thought about that. The grace of forgiveness was something he hadn't been able to give to his own brother. What did that make him?

It didn't take much in the way of detecting skills to know their world had been rocked at the resident nursing home. He spotted Fergie's so-called unmarked car parked in the lot, and the front lobby was empty. Walking down the hall, he heard chatter coming from Maury's open door. He paused by Cindi's door and tapped lightly.

The door opened at once. She must have been standing right behind it.

"Can I come in?" he whispered.

She nodded and waved him in with some urgency. She closed the door so quickly behind him that he had to take a couple of quick steps to get out of the way.

"Any idea what's going on down there?" he asked.

"Someone broke into his room. I tried to go in and help, but they shooed me away—Gladys and that whooping crane of a detective lady."

"Long red hair?"

"That's the one."

"Well, I just wanted to make sure you were okay since you were one of the ones who knew Maury so well."

"Yeah, one of the ones."

He had started to turn and head for the door. But he paused and waited.

Her voice quivered. "You know, when someone as young as Maury comes to a place like this, where there are about twenty ladies to any gentleman, it's quite a scramble at first to see who can get their hooks into the fresh man. I felt lucky and honored, for a while, until I found I was sharing."

Al nodded and took another step toward the door, afraid the record was going to get stuck.

"A lot of the ladies said Maury was a taker. Well, he was. And he took again, and again, and again. My stars. It's a wonder there was any of the man left. When you take that much, it's really a form of giving, don't you think?"

He nodded and made it to the door and out into the hallway before she could tell enough to leave him needing therapy through the years ahead. At the open door to Maury's room, he tapped before stepping in. Fergie was the first to spot him. She stood next to Gladys on the far side of the room, towering over the woman. Walsh was down on one knee, poking through a litter of mostly broken shells.

"It's a damned shame," Fergie said, "and I'll just bet Maury will be crying when he hears. But we don't think whoever did this got anything."

"Yeah," Walsh said. He held an open notepad on which he'd been taking notes. "The search has no ending spot, so whoever was in here didn't get anything." He looked up at Al, his eyes excited.

Al had seen that kind of enthusiasm at a crime scene

105

before, in his own eyes when he chanced past a mirror. Walsh was enjoying himself. The thrill of the chase was on. There was nothing like the first moments of nosing around, and while Maury's room looked as if it promised little, a detective could never know. Something might tie to Angel's death. Fergie had told Al that Walsh had a real nose for solving cases, so if there was anything to find there, he'd find it.

"It's still so awful. I feel so... so invaded," Gladys said.

Fergie stepped carefully as she wove through the room and made her way to the door. "Can we have a moment outside, Al?" She pulled Al into the hallway to drill him with the intensity of her violet-eyed stare. "You didn't think calling me might be a courtesy?"

"I wanted to, more than you might know."

She blushed. "Okay, then."

"What with my house being set on fire and Maury coming around and being half a step from needing to get popped with a tranquilizer dart, and what with finding a new place to hole up, I've had my hands full."

"Where are you going to be?"

"Maybe I shouldn't tell you."

"Okay." She took half a step back. "Well, okay then."

"Don't get huffy. I'm going to have to move around. When I get us settled, I'll call you first thing. Okay?"

She glanced down the hall then bent to kiss him on the cheek. "That's better." She straightened. "Oh. You'd better have this back." She dug in her jacket pocket and brought out Maury's little black book.

He took it from her. "Don't you need it?"

"I made a list of all the names and addresses. And you were spot on about the key players. They were all the ones you visited first. How did you do that?"

He didn't know what to make of her eyebrow raised in

mild amazement. "Those names had a small 'g.c.' beside them. Stands for 'golden cowry,' Maury's top marks for a woman."

"They must be so quietly proud to be rated."

"That reminds me. Wait here." He stepped inside Maury's room.

Gladys and Walsh were talking. They ignored him. He bent over and picked up a golden cowry from where it had rolled out across the rug. It was okay, not a scratch.

He went back out into the hall and showed it to Fergie. "Can I take this?"

"I don't care. Are you trying to make nice with your brother? That's good to hear."

He slipped the shell into his pocket beside the black book. "Will you talk to all the others in his book?"

"Have already. Nothing noteworthy you don't already know."

"The addresses were mostly women, but only three got the cowry rating."

She tilted her head, those striking eyes of hers lasering into his. "Mostly?"

"Well, I've got to get back to Maury. Bonnie's got her hands full."

"Can she handle him by herself?"

"I loaned her a Taser and told her if he got fresh, to light him up like the Christmas tree in Rockefeller Plaza."

She nodded. "That should do it."

He leaned closer, rose up on his toes, and kissed her cheek. "I've got to get going." He turned and started to walk away.

She called after him, "Hey, did you ever hear any rumors that Barrett might be a little bent?"

Al stopped and looked back at her. "What do you mean 'a little bent'?"

"I mean crooked as a pig's tail."

"Barrett?"

She shrugged. "How would you have handled that?"

"I don't know. It's hard to deal with your partner about stuff like that. I'm glad I never had to face that. It's not the sort of thing where you want to rat him out to internal affairs. Fortunately, it never came up. Barrett was a good partner, and though he could be a bit of a blockhead, he was straight as they come. Didn't have brains enough to be crooked and wouldn't have been if he could."

She nodded and went back into Maury's room.

He hurried down the hall, eager to get back to the houseboat.

———◆———

Once Al got his truck clear of the usual Austin traffic trying to tie itself into knots, the drive was enjoyable. He liked routine chores—like driving the truck, taking a shower, mowing the lawn—in which his motor cortex was occupied enough for his brain to clip along in comfortable free fall and sort things out.

He went through a couple of S-curves up one side of a hill and was going down the other side when he pulled the truck off the road and eased to a stop. He reached into the glove box and took out the small SureFire flashlight that took lithium batteries. It was too much light for the job, but he tugged out the black book and went through every page again.

When he was done, he rocked back in his seat. "Well, damn it all to hell!"

He pulled back onto the road, the lights of other vehicles strobing his way as each flickered past. He gripped the wheel tightly with both hands. The joy slipped gradually

TO HELL AND GONE IN TEXAS

away from the rest of the drive like air leaking out of a balloon.

By the time he parked by the houseboat, the sky was dark. He heard only the night sounds of creatures stirring and sounding off between the gusts of breeze that swayed the tops of trees like hula skirts. At least the air had cooled into the eighties.

He got his and Bonnie's bags out of the truck. On a whim, he took the Sig Sauer out of his bag and tucked it in at the small of his back. Listening intently, he examined every shadow all the way to the boat. As he walked across the gangplank, he saw that the marina crew had come and taken away his fishing boat to be dry-docked as he had asked.

Bracing for another of those always exciting rounds with Maury, he stepped onto the deck and went around to the glass sliding doors. He started to look inside. Behind him, he heard a gentle splashing.

Al turned and in the lights from the boat could make out some parts brown as a seal, and other parts not, as Bonnie swam playfully in the nude.

"Are you coming in or not?"

"Not." But he smiled. She *was* a tonic to be around.

"Give me one reason."

"Well, there's Fergie."

"Fuck Fergie." She splashed her way closer. "But I believe you've already done that."

"Still not coming in." He realized he was grinning in spite of himself.

"Then you'd better hand me that towel there by your feet."

He picked up the towel and held it out so she could come up and step into it. When she reached the ladder, he discreetly turned his head. When he looked again, she had the towel wrapped around her.

Her skin glistened wetly, and her grin was as wide and eager as any she'd shared so far. "That water felt *so* good."

"Where's Maury? You didn't have to fry him, did you?"

"Oh, he pouted a while about the notion I might Taser him. But I made him a sandwich and let him have one beer. He was anxious for real food. Then I sent him below. He must've had a day. I poked my head in to check on him, and he's as out of it as flapper dresses."

She spotted the small duffels he'd brought from the truck. "Oh, good. My stuff." She scooped up her bag, slid the glass door open, and dashed inside. "Uh oh. Al, you'd better come in here."

He picked up his bag and went inside. Two men sat waiting, one in a chair and the other on the bench at the dinette table. It looked as though they'd just slipped in while Bonnie was swimming and hadn't had a chance to look around yet. They didn't wear suits, but they smelled like feds to Al before he even got the door closed.

"How do you know we're not the bad guys?" the one sitting in the chair asked.

Al put down his bag. "Your hygiene, your diction, your posture, and that fact that neither one of you has even once glanced at Bonnie, and she's half hanging out of that towel. So who are you?"

"I'm Al," the one in the chair said.

"And I'm Maury," the other said.

"Or, if you prefer, I'm Tinker."

"And I'm Evers."

"You left out Chance," Al said.

"We never leave anything to chance," the one in chair said.

"Okay, knock it off. I'm gonna need to see some ID. I take it the ICE men have cometh." Al held out a hand.

They fished out their credentials and handed them over. Al glanced down. *Yep, they're ICE.*

"Terry O'Brien and Victor Zapata," Al read out loud for Bonnie. He passed the IDs back, and they tucked their leather folders away. He looked at Victor, the one in the chair. "What do you want?"

"We're here to tell you that we're not the ones you have to worry about. We're just here to warn you about the ones who should concern you. Some very dangerous hombres," Victor said.

"They'll have to find us."

"No worries there," Terry said. "We did."

CHAPTER THIRTEEN

"WE CAUGHT UP WITH YOUR friend Pinky just south of the Utah border," Victor said. "We had to threaten her a bit, but she knew her ass was on the line for poking around in places she shouldn't have hacked. We let them go on their merry way, but she had to bargain you up in exchange."

"That'll be reflected in her tip," Al said.

"The language those women used." Terry shook his head. "Like a couple of sailors. Kids didn't seem to mind, though. Probably heard it all before."

"Perhaps we should set a context for what's going on, in case you're in the dark about that." Victor had only the tiny vestigial remains of an accent, just enough to add exotic to his being dangerous. He had dark hair, unblinking brown eyes, and a face that looked as if he'd added some serious tanning time to his natural tone.

"You see," Terry said, "there's a war going on out there, and its name is terrorism." He'd probably rehearsed that line and said it before, often. His red hair was buzzed almost to the skin. He looked like someone who spent most of his time in the gym, pressing weights and staying as pale as the day he was born.

Al sighed. Something was off about the way the two were acting.

"A lot of Americans don't know it, but they're helping finance terrorism." Victor's stare swung from Al to Bonnie.

"Get outta here," Bonnie said.

Victor didn't even wince. "Every day, terrorists across the globe are being financed by Americans. Care to know how it's happening?"

Al knew a spiel aimed to wave the flag of patriotism when he heard it. But he waited, wanting to figure out why these guys were taking the long way around. The FBI agents he'd met were curt, abrupt to the point of being rude. Everything was on a need-to-know basis, and there was very little of that. One had told him the bureau's mantra: first, say nothing; next, deny everything; finally, begin counter-allegations. Compared to that standard, the two men in front of him were absolute chatterboxes. He'd have to wait them out to see what their agenda really was, if they had one.

Victor nodded. "Every day across America, teams of boosters sweep along the highways and hit drug stores and other business, shoplifting on a grand scale, some with metal-lined bags to beat security devices. They sell to wholesalers who resell the products, and the money goes to support terrorist organizations like the Hezbollah, al Qaeda, and FARC-EP, the Revolutionary Armed Forces of Colombia–that's *Fuerzas Armadas Revolucionarias de Colombia – Ejército del Pueblo*. These are very bad people." Victor's accent began to peek through more as his tone grew more heated. "What is more, they have strong ties with even fiercer gangs, like *Mara Salvatrucha* and the Mexican Zetas, *Los Zetas*."

"I've never heard anything about this before," Bonnie said. "The gangs, yes, but not this terrorist stuff. It's in no news I've seen."

Victor's face flushed, and his hands tightened into fists.

Terry spoke up, keeping his gaze on Al and ignoring Bonnie's remark. "It's the Zetas you need to worry about. They're the ones behind the mess that leads all the way to your brother."

"How so?" Al asked.

Victor gave him a tight-lipped smile. "Well, to tell the truth, Maury's a pretty insignificant cog in a big machine, one that is getting cleaned out by some of its competition, in a permanent way." He seemed to enjoy saying that. "There are a number of places stolen drugs were being sent by the *Mara Salvatrucha*. They get some dumb shit to receive packages, and he passes those on to another person who sells them. The dupe probably thinks it's harmless, just a few hundred Viagra, and he makes enough chicken feed to get by but not enough to matter to anyone. The thing is, all these gangs, cartels, and mafia are all in competition. They're businesses, but they can give a whole new meaning to hostile takeover. When the Zetas want to mess with someone else's distribution channels, they just start erasing the loose ends. If they get their hands on the right data, then they know where all those loose ends are."

"We think they've done just that, gotten their hands on a lot of that kind of detail," Terry said. "And a whole lot of erasing is going on. A whole family in Houston got rubbed out. Their pets, too. A guy in San Antonio came floating down past the River Walk on a loose barge. He was in about thirty-seven pieces, except his head, which was missing. And there are going to be a lot more killings."

A little light pinged on in Al's head. The only place he'd heard about where data like that was stored had been what Pinky had found in the federal files. Al had a niggling hunch an ICE investigation was what had started that particular ball rolling toward what was going wrong, but he kept his mouth shut and waited for them to finish.

"The thing is, we don't care much one way or the other about Maury," Victor said. "He could live, or he could die. We want whoever he worked with so we can work back to the source from that. You have to help us with that."

Al raised one eyebrow. "Have to?"

"Look," Terry said, "the thing is, we don't have a warrant or anything and don't even want to take Maury in. We just want to talk with him."

"And do what? Waterboard him?"

Victor shook his head. "No. Just talk. We were open with you just now. Transparent, the way our boss insists we be."

"Jaime Avila. Is he your boss?"

They looked toward each other, then back at Al.

"You know him?" Terry asked.

"I know him. We don't trade Christmas cards or anything. But I know him."

Victor shook his head. "Ah, because you were a big-shot sheriff's department detective. Right?"

"I don't like your tone, Victor. I get the impression you don't think much of someone in that position, or recently retired from it."

"Well..." Victor said, dragging out the word, "always good for maybe becoming a security guard at Walmart."

A long moment stretched out where the wake of a passing boat that ignored the No Wake signs sent the houseboat rocking in its mooring. Waves slapped against the hull in a rhythmic pattern that might have been lulling at any other time.

"Now, we want to see your brother." Terry frowned, all his patience used up.

"What about?" Maury stood in the open doorway of the stairs that led down to the lower stateroom. He wore the same khaki slacks, loafers, and burgundy shirt, but he'd somehow managed to get out most of the wrinkles. That made him look more presentable.

Both Victor and Terry jumped to their feet. Victor was quite a bit shorter than Terry, but Al still regarded him as the one to watch.

When Victor's hand slid toward his holster, Al said, "Stand down on any hardware. You want to talk, then talk." Al held his Sig Sauer down at his side.

Terry's eyes widened. "Really? You're gonna pull a weapon on federal agents?"

"No one's done anything like that." Al stared each of them down. "Let's say I'm looking into a couple of trespassers. We'll see how the next few moments go. You want to speak to him. Do it."

Terry turned back to Maury. "Will you tell us who you were working with?"

"No." Maury glanced at Al.

"I got the same answer from him," Al said. "And I was as thrilled about it as you are. But you've had your talk. Maybe there's another way for you to get your homework done. Until you come back with a warrant and a better hand to play—one with cards all from the same deck—I'm gonna ask you to get the hell off this boat. Now!"

Victor looked like a snake ready to strike. His mouth opened, but before he could say anything, Terry grabbed his arm and tugged him toward the door. They filed out, and Al followed to make sure they crossed the gangplank to shore. He watched them until they climbed into their vehicle, one of those ubiquitous black SUVs. When the engine started and they pulled away, he waited until it was out of sight, and then he brought in the gangplank.

116

He came back into the room. "You'd better get ready to untie us, Bonnie. I'm firing up the engine. We're about to change locations."

"I can't believe you stood up for me," Maury said.

"Me neither." Al winked toward Bonnie. "Now, step lively."

"Do you really know their boss, this Jaime fellow?" she asked.

"I saved his life once, back when he was FBI. Well, I let him know his wife was coming home from Europe early. We both think she shot her first husband, and Jaime was giving her grounds to do the same to him."

Bonnie shook her head. "What is it with you men?"

"You should talk. You were willing to bonk me just a short while ago."

"I'd like to see that," Maury said.

"Come on, people. We'll have plenty of time to trade lies once we're someplace else on this lake."

Bonnie pulled her towel tighter around herself, grabbed her bag, and headed down the stairs to the main stateroom where she'd have more privacy to change.

"Hey, Al?"

"What, Maury?"

"Thanks."

"It's always a good idea to piss off as many federal agents as you can in a day."

"I mean it. Thanks."

"Forget about it. You'd have done the same for me."

CHAPTER FOURTEEN

A L STOOD ON THE BACK deck, putting out a line from the corner of the houseboat. He twirled the baited hook and weight in a steady circle and then let go. The line shot out and landed with a *plonk* as the weight splashed in and carried the line swiftly toward the bottom.

He looked out across the still water where he could see rings spreading from half a dozen places where fish had come up to the surface to feed. The rocky shore was fifteen feet away. He glanced up the forty-foot-tall limestone cliff face next to them. Nothing stirred, except the ends of the green ferns where spring water dripped down through the fronds. Tight lines went out, one from the stern and one from the bow, keeping the houseboat snug in its cove.

He slid the glass door open and went inside. Bonnie was clanking around with a skillet and an aluminum coffee percolator—real camping sort of hardware. She started pulling out eggs and bacon from the fridge.

"Hey, I can do that," he said.

"Naw. I don't mind. It kinda calms me and gives me something to do."

He went to the fridge and took out a cantaloupe. Using his fish-filleting knife, he split the melon, deseeded it with a spoon, and cut it into eighths. Then all he had to do was feather the knife along between rind and meat, slice the orange crescent moons into bite-sized pieces, and drop those into a bowl.

Bonnie had the skillet popping and sending the smell of bacon through the boat—one of the finest smells ever to be part of a morning.

The hatch door to the lower stateroom opened, and Maury came out. "Well, aren't you two a cozy domestic scene."

"We live to serve," Al said. "You know me. I get restless if I'm not doing something."

"And I'm rested because someone doesn't want to do something with me." Bonnie bounced her hip into the side of Al's leg.

"No one asked me," Maury said.

"And no one's gonna." She flipped the bacon then glanced at Maury. "You *are* looking a sight better than you were. How're you feeling?"

"Better than I have in quite a while. The sea air must agree with me."

"We're not at sea." Al frowned, wishing he'd said nothing.

Maury stretched out his arms. "Being on the water must agree with me, then."

"I'll take your vitals in a minute," Bonnie said, "soon as I finish whipping us up some nourishment. Did you pick up OJ, Al?"

"Sure. Enough for a day or two." Maury shook his head at the two of them being so domestic and stepped outside, sliding the door closed behind him.

It did all sound a little cozy. *He won't be thinking that in a while.* Al shook his head.

"How much time do you think we have at this spot?" Bonnie spoke softly.

"Can you read minds?"

119

"No. I just have some notion of the pickle we're in, and it could get a whole lot worse."

"I expect we have a day, maybe a day and a half."

"Are we just going to sit here and wait?"

"I don't know yet. I'll have to think on it."

"Well, let me know when you've thunk."

Later that morning, Bonnie and Maury came out onto the deck, carrying three folding chairs. Al finished doing his pushups, stood, and grabbed for his T-shirt. He tugged it on while they opened the chairs.

"How are you feeling?" Al asked Maury. "Fit and hale enough now to move around if we have to?"

"Okay, I guess. But I doubt I could do a tenth of the pushups you just did. How many was it?"

"Ten. I just try to hedge the bet against the inroads made by the years badly spent."

Maury chuckled.

Bonnie winked at Al. "I don't know, Maury. Given your hobbies, maybe you're the one who should be out here doing pushups."

"Oh, Al has always been the gym rat of us. His strong work ethic has driven him in his work as well as his exercise. He thinks everything in life has to have a purpose."

Al could have added that Maury's way had always been to seek the easiest path and coast along it. Yet his brother's physical condition belied that notion. He looked as though he'd been rode hard and put away wet. About all they could do was feed him well and hope he was up to a scramble, if it came to that.

"All through high school, Maury had a favorite shirt—one covered in bright cartoons. A real chick magnet, he called it. His favorite of the 'toons was a panel that read,

'Meanwhile, miles away, Pierre was driving aimlessly.' Above Pierre's head, as he drove an open-topped convertible, was a bubble that read, 'I'm driving aimlessly.'"

"It's still funny," Maury said.

Al looked out across the lake. The breeze had picked up, and a chop of wave sets swept across the mouth of their small cove. Out on the lake proper, short whitecaps marked the tips of bigger waves. That didn't slow the occasional pair of jet skiers or water skiers who whooshed past. The wakes from their crafts reached the houseboat and rocked it in place.

"Now *those* people know how to have fun," Maury said.

Al was still getting used to the notion of talking back and forth, sharing ideas and opinions. It had been so long since he and his brother had talked at all. Al had often thought about fun, pleasure, and enjoyment. Out on the boat, he'd always acknowledged how good it was to be on the water, even if the fishing wasn't all it could be. In the quiet nights alone, playing chess or reading a book, with a fire going in the fireplace, he'd been pretty happy. Maury probably had a whole different spin on what it meant to feel alive and... well, happy.

Bonnie sat up in her chair and pointed. "Hey, one of your lines is tight, Al."

Al went over to the corner of the boat and pulled on the line. It gave a head shake back, so he began to pull it in, hand over hand. As it neared the boat the catfish's efforts got more vigorous. He could see it now. A sleek channel cat, about a two-pounder. He slung the fish onto the deck, where it flopped around vigorously. When it bounced toward Maury, he got up from his chair and moved away.

Al chuckled. "Ah, that's right. Maury was never much of a fisherman." He got his hand under the catfish's belly, lifted it, and held it still while he removed the hook. He put the catfish into a fish basket he'd found in the stowage compartment where he'd gotten the line. Then, he tied one end of its tender line to a cleat and dropped the basket over the side where it could float beside the houseboat.

"You're halfway to lunch," Bonnie said. "Catch another one."

Al baited the hook with half a strip of uncooked bacon and heaved out the line. "You want to tell her *your* fishing experience, Maury?"

"I'd rather not and say I did."

"Let's just say the sport is not his métier. But he did catch something far bigger than I just did."

Maury sighed. "Must we go into this?"

Al wasn't about to stop. "Our grandfather drove us to a creek, with old-fashioned cane poles tied to the side of his blue Studebaker. We had to tiptoe through a field of cow pies to get to this pool with a sand bank. Maury had trouble getting his worm on his hook because he didn't want to hurt it. He was trying to tie it in a knot."

Bonnie's shoulders started to shake. Maury glared at her, then at Al.

"The real excitement came when he went to make an overhand cast and the hook swung upward and sank into the seat of his jeans. He screamed, 'A fish has me. A fish has me,' and he ran straight out into the pool. Messed up the fishing for a spell, but grandpa and I were laughing too hard to fish right then anyway."

Bonnie pointed at the line. "Hey, you've got another one. Let me pull it in. Okay?"

"Sure." He liked her hearty enthusiasm. She was bouncy and full of pep. She wouldn't be the problem later.

Al glanced at Maury and almost asked him how he was feeling again. His brother looked a little better with more color in his cheeks and some glitter to his eyes. But Al probably wasn't going to be able to count on him for any of the heavy lifting when things got dicey. Not if, but when.

Bonnie hauled the flopping fish up onto the deck. It was twice as big as the one Al had caught. She grinned like someone who'd just won a dozen lotteries.

Al cleaned the two fish and put the fillets in a bowl of salted water in the fridge. He pulled in the lines and stowed them.

Bonnie and Maury were chattering away when he came back out on the back deck.

"I'll get those fried up for lunch," Al said. "First, I have to make a call, and you two might as well hear what you can of it."

He punched in the number from memory. His was the sort of mind that collected and held on to scraps of information. Usually the less valuable the information, the more likely he was to retain it. In this case, knowing the number was handy. The phone was picked up on the second ring.

"Jaime, you old dog you. What have you been up to?"

"Just sitting by the fire listening to stories, Al. One was that a couple of my boys said you pulled a gun on them."

"Really? That doesn't sound like me. I doubt I'd do anything like that unless I caught them trespassing or something."

"Hmm."

"Are those two a couple of your rising stars?"

"Why do you ask?"

"They seemed like overzealous young bucks running maverick and trying to make names for themselves. Usually, organizations like yours hire carefully, but you must get all types. Most work out, I'll bet, but some probably don't. You've had to add a lot of agents lately, and in a hurry."

"Well, truth be told, Al, the jury is still out on these two. I can't say much. But sometimes they get quick results. Other times not. What made them ping on your sonar?"

"I never heard federal agents talk as much as those two did. They spun some overripe cow plonk I wouldn't have tried on a first-year deputy, much less an old out-to-pasture case like me."

"That sounds like them all right. It's sure not like the old days anymore. What is it you want from me?"

"What can you tell me about the bad wind that's blowing this way?"

"That it's as bad as you've ever seen."

"Zetas? In all the smoke and mirrors your guys were heaving my way, I couldn't be sure."

"You've got it, and a bad lot of them at that. The Zetas got hold of data about their *Mara Salvatruchas* competition, out to the tiny end strings of the network, like Maury. They have a team out doing some serious erasing. They're the ones we want. Osiel Cárdenas Santiago's the cell leader. The two men with him on the cleanup squad are Flavio "the Machete" Méndez and Eduardo Soto Tlapanco. Flavio is the knife man. Eduardo is the muscle, the gunner, and the one with a kink for torture. Well, hell, I guess you have to put Flavio down for that, too."

"You think these are the sort who'd kill a three-legged deer just to be messing around?"

"They killed Three-legged Bob?" Bonnie asked, jumping up out of her chair.

"They're exactly that sort," Jaime said. "Is Maury and that nurse still with you?"

"Yep. That was Bonnie you heard yelping."

"Well, I appreciate you calling me, Al. Anything else?"

"No. That's it for now." Al hung up and put the cell phone back in his pocket.

Bonnie had not sat back down. "I can't believe anyone

would catch and kill a poor deer that had survived having only three legs."

"I did feel pretty lousy about it. I'm glad you understand." Al looked over at Maury. Some of the color had slid from his brother's face. The sun was beaming down on them, but Al didn't think that was all that was causing the sweat to bead on Maury's brow.

"I... I've made a right mess of it for a lot of people, haven't I? I can't quit thinking about Angel. Tortured and dead." Maury rubbed his forehead.

"I think it's time we went inside and checked you again from stem to stern." Bonnie reached out and gave Maury's elbow a tug.

Maury got up, and she led him over to the door.

Maury turned back to Al. "Look, I don't know if I ever said this before, or as intensely as I mean it now, but I'm sorry. I'm truly sorry for all I've fucked up in your life and in everyone else's around me. I feel like... well, I know I'm like some tragic curse, and it's not brought on by any cosmic source but is all my own doing. For that, I'm truly, truly sorry." He bowed his head and let himself be tugged by Bonnie.

Al shook his head and put his hands in his pockets. He touched Maury's golden cowrie and decided he'd tell his brother about a good many of his precious shells getting broken later. At the moment, Maury seemed fragile, much too fragile, and that wasn't going to help with whatever boom was about to lower onto them.

He sat and watched the other boats, the waves, and the clouds drifting into one shape then another. The mottle of the sky reflected as a leprosy of splotches on the sides of the waves. Al wondered, for the longest time, if he had the brass himself to apologize the way Maury had for his own share of being far from perfect.

CHAPTER FIFTEEN

AL NUDGED MAURY'S SHOULDER. HIS brother stirred slightly and pulled the bed covers closer. Bonnie reached out and pulled the bedspread back.

Maury's eyes snapped open. "What?"

"We've got to go. Now." Al kept his voice to a near whisper, but made sure the urgency came through.

Maury grumbled, pushed the covers off, and stood, wearing a pair of white jockey underwear. His legs and arms were scrawny. His belly and chest had some sag, but there wasn't enough of him to droop too much. His skin, where not tanned dark on his face and arms, was the color of tired cooked egg whites, covered with a light matting of greying fur—all around, a far cry from *Playgirl* centerfold material. Maybe some of that was behind his moving to a nursing home.

Maury scratched his butt and picked up his pants from the floor. "I don't suppose I could ask for a little privacy."

"I'm a nurse," Bonnie said. "I've seen things that'd make you want to tear your eyes out. Now, hurry. Al says we gotta be outta here pronto."

"And I don't suppose you can tell me what's going on. Right?" Maury pulled on the only shirt he'd worn for the past few days.

Al held out a pair of worn jogging shoes. "Here. See if a

pair of my sneakers will fit you. We used to be about the same size."

Maury frowned, but he took them and sat on the corner of the bed to put them on. "Now what?"

"Let's go." Al flipped the light switch. "We'll go in the dark from here on."

"How can we—ow!" Maury mumbled.

"Just stay close," Al said. "It'll seem lighter once we get outside."

"What time is it?"

"Don't worry about that. It's dark. That's what we were waiting for."

"Hey. Cut that out," Bonnie said.

Maury chuckled. "Just making sure it was you."

"You don't have to do so by Braille. Keep your distance or you're gonna see some lights. There'll be stars at first, and then you won't see anything."

As soon as they were out on the deck, Al could see better. The dim glow of the half-moon reflecting off the water lit the area enough for him to guide his companions over to the ladder that led down to the water. Al handed each of them a square life preserver and took one himself. He started down the ladder.

"We're just going to get in the water? No boat, or anything?" Maury whispered.

"Chances are we will get wet," Al said, already up to his waist in the water. "Now, step lively."

"Have you really thought this all the way out?"

"Shh."

The soft splashing of each of them entering the water were the only sounds they made for the next few seconds. A natural-enough sound in the night.

Al moved closer to Bonnie. "Grab the strap on the

preserver I'm holding, and let the other end of yours trail back for Maury to hang onto."

Through clenched teeth, Maury said, "My god, this water's cold. I think I'm starting to get hypothermia already. I'm shaking."

"Can you swim, Maury?" Bonnie asked.

"Hang on now. I'm starting for the shore," Al said. "Yes, he can swim." Al spoke in as soft a whisper as he could manage. He was aware of how sound carried across water, and he would have preferred silence all the way to shore. But Maury sounded ready to have a panic attack, and that might infect Bonnie. "When we were kids, our mother decided that it would be a good idea if Maury and I learned to swim. She took us out to a resort at a freshwater lake where the water was as brown as coffee with cream. The bottom was more mud than sand, and we were constantly stepping on the sharp edges of large clams. And as it turned out, all the other kids were half our age, so we towered over all of them. I think it was the only time in our lives that we were that much bigger than our peers."

Maury sighed. "It was like being pro basketball centers."

"The instructor, a heavy-set Amazonian girl named Hilga, leaned to the Mussolini school of doing things. She ordered us to pair off into buddies and keep an eye on the other person. Of course, Maury and I were stuck with each other. The minute Hilga turned away, Maury and I both dove underwater and swam as hard as we could until we came out under a floating dock and some forty feet away. Neither of us were much good at swimming on top of water, but we both could swim like otters underwater. We treaded water under the dock, hanging on and watching Hilga get more and more frantic as she looked for us. She was slapping the water and yelling. We got kicked out of the class for giving her a near coronary, but it was some of the most fun we ever had." He almost added, "together," but left that off.

He could see the cliff nearing as he tugged the life preserver with one hand and side-stroked with his other arm, leading his little caravan to the rip rap of loose rocks that marked the shore at the base of the cliff. As soon as he felt the beginning of the jagged edges of the stones that made up the bottom, Al tugged harder, bringing them along, until he was close enough to take careful steps forward. He pulled himself up onto the shore, an uneven stretch of rock and rubble mostly worn smooth through the years, then turned and got hold of both of Bonnie's hands and hauled her up next to him. Then he did the same for Maury. His brother opened his mouth to say something, but Al shushed him. He led them across the smoothed way until they stood at the base of the cliff.

"How in the world are we going to climb that?" Maury asked, as he dripped up close enough to Al to whisper.

"Way ahead of you, Maury. I came over earlier and set this up." Al stepped close to the cliff and tugged a rope free that he'd tucked into a crevice.

Maury looked up the sheer side of the cliff. "You want us to climb that? How?"

"I've made a harness. I'm going to send you up first, then Bonnie. About two thirds of the way up, there's a small shelf, like a cave that juts in below an overhang. I fixed a pulley to the trunk of a bald cypress. When you get to the cave, send the harness back down and wait in there."

"Is this really necessary? I'm wet. It'll be cold."

"I put three blankets up there. You'll be fine. Now, get into this harness."

"Are you quite sure?" Maury gave the rope a slight tug.

129

"This doesn't seem like a very thick rope. Is it rigged well? I mean so it's safe?"

"Actually, Maury, I'm rather proud to have been able to rig anything like it at all from what I was able to find on the boat. And, yes, it's safer than staying here."

"Well, let me go on record as not fully sharing in your enthusiasm. If this thing snaps and breaks my neck, I'm never speaking to you again."

"Promises. Promises."

Al started fitting Maury into the harness. He couldn't see far, but the advantage was that anyone else—unless they were wearing first-rate night-vision goggles—wouldn't be able to see, either. The mournful hoot of an owl mixed with other rustles and night sounds. A breeze rustled some dried leaves around the base of the cliff. In the distance, the low sound of a boat's motor burbled slowly as it came their way.

"Hurry." Al heaved on his end of the rope. Maury rose off the ground and up the cliff's side like a reluctant spider being pulled to its web. After a few moments, the rope went slack, and Al brought the harness down. Bonnie stepped up, and he helped her get strapped in. He began hauling on the rope, and she went up a few feet then stopped. He tugged. The pulley felt stuck. He reached up and pushed on Bonnie's rump with one hand while pulling on the rope with the other. She started up again, but not before she'd wiggled her rump on Al's hand. He could hear her quietly giggling as she rose up to the indentation to join Maury.

When the rope slackened again, Al brought down the harness and got into it. He tied the loose end to his belt. That was just for safety. He'd pretty much have to rock-climb up the cliff freestyle, but he'd done it earlier, so he could do it again.

He went from handhold to foothold, picking his way

with care and testing each hold before depending on it. When he pulled himself up over the lip of the cave, there was barely room for him. He drew up the loose loop of rope and coiled it.

"Climb over me," Bonnie said. "I'm not gonna lay here next to the man with a thousand hands. He was hogging all the blankets, too. Watch yourself settling in, though. Some tomfool has put a plastic bag with guns and ammo right in the middle here."

Al climbed over her and settled into place between them. The weapons bag he placed by his head like a lumpy pillow. He took out the Sig and slipped it into his pocket, hoping Bonnie wouldn't have any wise-ass remarks if it pressed against her in the night.

"Do you want to hold one of the guns in case things get busy, Maury?" Al asked.

"Absolutely not."

"I'll take it," Bonnie said. "My daddy spent weeks teaching me to shoot. He said if I ever caught my husband with someone, I wouldn't want to miss and hit the wrong one. I got pretty good at hitting cans but never did figure out what he meant by the wrong one. I planned on giving them both a third eye if that ever happened. All kidding aside, I'm hotter than a tater tot with about any peashooter you hand me—a fact that didn't escape my ex's attention. I just hope some raccoon doesn't decide to try and burgle this cave."

It was quiet in the cave for a few moments, with just the soft rustling of them pulling their blankets close around their wet clothes.

Maury broke the silence. "I'm freezing. Are we really going to try to stay here? Why?"

"Maury, we're going to have to be as still as we can from now on." Al pulled his now-damp blanket closer. He lay with his back to Maury. Bonnie had her blanket around her but had backed closer to Al as soon as he was settled.

"Isn't this nice? Spooning."

"Shh, Maury."

Bonnie reached back and took Al's right wrist, brought it around her. "Don't let me fall out. Okay?"

He mumbled an okay.

She moved his arm. "Put your hand there."

Al tried to pull his hand back. "Bonnie..."

She held tight. "Squeeze a bit, if you like."

Behind him, Maury groaned.

"Tell us a story, Al," Bonnie said.

"Shh. Everyone. Quiet from now on."

For the longest time, Al didn't think he would sleep at all, even though he should have been the most tired of the three. He lay listening to the sounds of waves lapping the shore, the soft regular creaking from the houseboat, the sounds of night birds, some with their cries and the wings of others fluttering past outside the cave.

As the night stretched on, Bonnie began to snore softly, then Maury. The air got cooler, and the stone seemed to try to suck every bit of warmth from him. In her sleep, Bonnie nestled back closer.

Al tried thinking of Fergie, felt part of himself stirring. *Bad idea.* He went for a blank mind, concentrating on his own breathing, though he didn't think he'd ever fall asleep.

Then he awoke to the sound of gunfire. Al raised his head to look over Bonnie. He saw flashes of light coming from inside the boat, accompanying each shot. Some came one by one, others in bursts. Bonnie started to sit up, and he gently pressed her back down.

"What's going on?" Maury whispered.

"Shh." Al could feel Bonnie trembling, either from the

cold or from the knowledge they could have been down in that boat.

"If we're not there, why's anyone shooting?" Maury asked.

"Quiet, Maury. Please don't make another sound. I mean it."

"Just tell me—"

Al rammed his elbow back into Maury's stomach. They lay there like three corpses, though Bonnie trembled, and Maury breathed strenuously. The shooting below stopped at last, followed by shouting, in Spanish. A boat's motor started and pulled away, now going as flat out as its big motor could go.

CHAPTER SIXTEEN

A L, MAURY, AND BONNIE STOOD on the deck of the sheriff's department boat. They'd been given dry, warm blankets, but all three of them were still shivering. Spotlights lit up the houseboat, making it the glowing centerpiece in the black of night. With the bright lights on, Al could no longer make out any features in the sky. Maury and Bonnie both hunched their shoulders and clutched their blankets, looking like a couple of winter birds riding out a blizzard. Al heard the sound of a helicopter approaching in the distance.

"That'll be Jaime," Sheriff Clayton said. "He'll have his back feathers up, don't you think?"

Wayon Gallard came out onto the deck of the houseboat, into the harsh glare from the spotlights. He waved to the sheriff.

"Wait on Jaime before you do anything," Clayton called to him. "He'll want a first look."

Al looked up toward the approaching light and roar of helicopter blades. "You get anything on the boat that peeled out of here?"

Clayton shook his head. "Like as not, it was stolen. We'll hear in the morning, when it's too late to do anything. We don't even know where to set up any roadblocks even if we had the men to do that."

"Where's he going to land?" Al asked, nodding up toward the chopper.

"You'll see. He's just had two agents popped. It's a wonder he even needs a copter. Wayon says it's a real bloodbath in there. Feds like the FBI may seem ploddish and overly careful to us. Some of these ICE guys are a whole new breed. They have to be."

"They were brash, overconfident young men. Like a lot of young people, they probably thought they were bulletproof. But no one should have to die like that." Al shook his head.

"And you three just happened to be hid out up on the hill while it all went down. Right?"

"We didn't think there'd be anyone in the boat for those guys to find."

"Doesn't look like you'll be getting your deposit back when you return this boat."

"That doesn't matter a hill of beans just now."

"Zetas, Jaime tells me," Clayton said.

A rope ladder dropped from the bottom of the chopper. A man started climbing down it while the helicopter was still lowering into place. As soon as the end of the ladder neared the deck, Jaime Avila hopped off onto the deck, and the ladder was reeled up. The chopper rose and flew away.

Jaime strode over to the sheriff, an angry scowl on his face, his eyes flickering sparks of light from the obsidian. He squinted up at Al as he shook his hand. "I'm glad you're okay. We're gonna talk when I've had a look."

Jaime Avila may have been four, even five inches shorter than Al, but there was nothing pint-sized about his intensity or passions. He reminded Al of a bullet, some tapered bronzed projectile shot out of a cannon. He wore a black ICE short-sleeved shirt, in deference to the weather,

135

and it fit tight enough to show off an awfully trim but muscled build for a man in the tail end of his forties. He stared into Al's eyes for a couple more seconds, as if scanning and recording, then spun and climbed down to be ferried over to the houseboat by one of the deputies in a smaller boat.

As Jaime boarded the houseboat and rushed inside the open sliding door, Sheriff Clayton leaned closer to Al. "Do you think he was using Maury for bait?"

Al nodded.

"Thought so. What'd you do, call him on your cell and let him get a GPS read on you?"

Al nodded again.

"Well, it's on his head then, but that isn't going to keep him from being madder than seventeen wet hens."

"I'll bet he's madder that the Zetas probably *had* to get the location from ICE. That means a leak somewhere."

"You put an operation worth billions up against an agency on the taxpayer's dole, and you've got a mismatch if the loyalty and trust runs out in even one individual."

Al nodded. Sure felt like he was doing a lot of nodding, but perhaps the rattle didn't bother Clayton.

"Wayon told me one of those agents lived long enough to be tortured." Clayton shook his bear-like head. "They cut off his fingers, one by one until they were all in a pile. I imagine he told them everything he knew and more. I mean when he still had his head."

Al started to ask a question. Clayton held up a hand for him to hold that thought. Jaime was coming back across in the department skiff. The sheriff moved closer to wait so they could have their head-to-head.

Bonnie sat down, slowly and carefully. She clutched her blanket tighter. Maury stood staring off across the water, as if there were answers there and they might well be sailing this way at any moment. He looked as pale as he ever had, and the cold accentuated his wrinkles. His discomfort made Al feel warmer toward him. They were both getting older and closer to the big finish. He'd always thought he'd beat Maury there, get shot or something, but now he wasn't so sure.

Al eased up beside Maury and looked in the same direction. The water appeared black on the surface, unfathomable. All the lights fixed on the houseboat had changed it. The hubbub going on had stilled all the night creatures, except for some bats that flittered about in jerky nervous circles around the edges of the light, taking advantage of a bonanza of insects in flight.

"Let me ask you something, Maury. You wouldn't give up the name of whoever you worked with, to me or to ICE. Why?"

"You're the one who always told me, Al, that if you have a partner, you don't drop a dime, no matter what. You're not their judge."

"What if the partner is as bent as a stepped-on pig's tail?"

"Still goes. Hell, it's your credo. I just borrowed it."

"Fair enough. I can't ask you to break what I've stressed far too often myself. Never rat out your partner, no matter what."

Another boat was coming their way. Al figured it was probably the medical examiner, one from the fed's side. It had been a long night so far, and it was shaping up to be an even longer one.

"Oh, there's this." Al dug into his pocket and pulled out the golden cowry shell. It was three inches long, round and smooth, and had a dark amber glow even in the bad light.

Maury reached out for it and grasped it.

"Be careful. Something was rattling in there."

"Did you...?"

"Yeah, I took a look. Seemed like a safety deposit box key to me."

Maury's head lowered but then snapped up. "Look, when all this is over, I can help you get your house fixed up like new. Okay?"

"I wouldn't take that kind of money from you, for one. You're going to need some of it anyway for replacing your shell collection. This was one of the few survivors."

"They smashed my shells? Why?"

"It's the sort of thing they do, like killing Three-legged Bob and Angel."

"You knew to save this one from the bunch, didn't you?"

"I know you," Al said. He stepped closer and lowered his voice. "Just so you know, those two headless ICE guys in there, cut up like so much hamburger now, weren't really interested in you or who your partner was, except how it helped them reel in who they were after. You were just the worm tied onto the hook, Maury. Just the worm."

Maury stared down at the shell in his hand. He didn't respond.

"Here's the thing, Maury. I'll be as honest as I can be. I don't know if I can save you... if I can save *us*. You're not worth putting into a witness protection program. Even if you were, I doubt Jaime wants to give you over to the Marshals. When these ICE guys are done talking to us, we'll walk out of here and have to face whatever comes next. My feeling is that it's going to be worse than the winds of hell. Much worse. I don't say this to scare you but just to let you know the dilemma we're facing. Okay? I'm telling you this to say I'm sorry now if I can't keep you alive, because I'm just starting to care for you again the way I always did."

Maury nodded then turned his head and rubbed a knuckle across his eye.

Al put his hand on Maury's shoulder. "Well, we may not have much time left between us, but what do you say we make the most of it?"

———◆———

The drive out to Lake Buchanan that night a few years back had been a long one, especially so late, and Al hadn't even been sure it would be worth his while. Still, it was a courtesy. His headlights cut swaths into the black, and just as he turned the corner off 29 onto Ranch Road 2341, they spotlighted a tight pack of coyotes that nearly spilled onto the road in front of him. They were fighting over something, teeth flashing in open jaws. Their hides were washed white in the harsh glare. The animals spun, saw the truck, and dispersed in all directions, like an asterisk, their tails hung low and their legs going fast.

Al caught a glimpse of what they'd been fighting over—what was left of an armadillo, just scraps of drying meat inside the plated husk of its armor. That summed up what kind of year the county was having. He drove on, thinking of the Texas saying, "Contrary to popular belief, all armadillos aren't born dead beside the road." He wasn't so sure about that. But he usually pulled the day shift. Dead was the only way he'd ever seen them.

He had called ahead and gotten the cabin number, so when he pulled up into the lot of the Canyon of the Eagles Lodge, he pulled his truck close to the right one. He let his headlights sweep across the closed drapes, announcing his arrival. He got out, went up to the door, and knocked, betting fifty-fifty on getting no answer.

He was about to turn and get back into the truck when the lock rattled. The door opened a crack. Jaime's face above a white terry robe pressed halfway into the opening, his right hand down and out of sight behind him.

"What in the hell do you want?" Jaime hissed. "More to the point, how in the devil did you know where I was?"

He glared at Al with a look Al had only seen once before in his life. Al had once gone along with a group of ranchers and two Texas Parks and Wildlife officers to supervise the safe capture and removal of a mountain lion that had been killing cattle. The dogs rushed on ahead with the men close after them, not thinking that the cat might have backtracked, gotten behind them. Al ran to catch up and heard a hiss. He looked up in a tree to his right and, six feet away, within springing distance, crouched the mountain lion on the bare limb of a dead pecan tree, its ears flat back, its mouth open with teeth showing, and its eyes the most intense mix of fear and anger at the same time Al had ever seen. The mountain lion had turned and fled, but that rare and complex mix of extreme emotion was what Al saw in Jaime's eyes, and he knew the man held a gun in that lowered hand.

"I'd be a pretty poor detective if I didn't know what was going on in my county," Al said.

"What is it you want?" Jaime hissed.

"I was at the airport, checking on some travelers who interested the department. I happened to be looking at flight records and saw that one of the passengers on a plane coming in the morning was a Diana Anne Avila. Last time I spoke to you, you said she wasn't due back until next week."

Al stood and watched it all register. It took a second or two for all the anger to slowly ebb and evaporate from the man's face.

Jaime blinked up at him. "Oh, well thanks." He closed the door.

On the way back to his home, Al had time to think about whether he'd done the right thing. He supposed he had. Usually it was none of his business whether men or women honored their marriage vows, unless it broke the law or hurt some innocent bystander. But if he'd let Jaime's wife catch and surprise him, knowing she may well have shot a previous husband, then Jaime's death would have been on his own head. That was not something he could have lived with. He did sleep very well when he finally climbed between the covers.

The approaching boat swung over beside the houseboat, dropped off the medical examiner, then came to the sheriff's department boat. A tall man in a black suit climbed onto the deck. He went straight to Jaime, and they settled into a huddle.

They both spoke with the sort of animated arm-waving Al expected of them, their faces close together. Al knew they'd decided something when their arms dropped to their sides and they came over to Sheriff Clayton. Jaime gestured for Al to join them. Al left Maury standing at the rail and walked over to the other men.

"This is Sergio Guerra Ramírez," Jaime said, "my lieutenant, right-hand man, and former partner."

Sergio's gaze passed over each of them, and seemed to be recording a great deal. His brown eyes didn't possess Jaime's animal intensity, but his penetrating look hinted at analytical skills that had to be just as useful on the ICE team. And there was no compassion whatsoever in his expression. Al had sat across a chessboard from faces like that often enough to recognize the type.

"And?" Clayton prodded.

"The best we can do is offer Al and his brother a safe

house in Austin. Sergio and I will be there to ensure nothing happens."

"But you do expect something to happen. Right?" Clayton said.

"It is possible. But we would seek to head it off, stop it." Jaime pursed his lips. At his height he had to look up to stare toward Clayton's face.

Whether he went with Sun Tzu's *The Art of War* or Bobby Fischer's book on chess, Al could sense someone setting up an endgame. He didn't care for the role he'd been cast, didn't care for it at all, but he didn't have much choice either. "Why does that make me feel like a block of cheese?" he asked.

Clayton tilted his head a half inch. "You're going to be able to stop them? You have enough manpower and firepower for that?"

"That's the idea." Jaime looked at Sergio. "You were on their heels in Houston and San Antonio, right?"

Sergio nodded. "We got there too late both times. Same thing with those Collier men in your county. Found messes like this." He nodded toward the houseboat. "This is the first chance we have to be one step ahead of them. We need to do this thing."

"I see. You could have it at an open farmhouse, but that'd be in the county, my turf." Clayton's voice lowered. "What's the probability they'll show?"

"It is likely," Jaime said.

"I don't like that." Al glanced toward Maury and Bonnie. They waited—wet, chilly, and with what looked like little patience.

"It's all we've got. We could ask the local police, the Boy Scouts, and the mail carriers all to help." Jaime was looking at him with less respect than Al was accustomed to. "Hell, you can drive yourself to the safe house if you like. Look, I'm doing this as a favor to you. What else do you want?"

Al glared at him. "Just don't pass me a buffalo chip and tell me it's a steak."

"Okay. It's not a steak."

"Thanks."

"Anything else?"

"Please don't do me any more favors."

"*That,* we can do!"

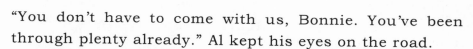

"You don't have to come with us, Bonnie. You've been through plenty already." Al kept his eyes on the road.

Sitting in the passenger seat, Bonnie reached out to pat Al's shoulder. "Hey, you two can't make it without your fearless sidekick. Besides, Maury still needs the care of a professional nurse. I am still on the clock too, aren't I?"

"Sure."

"Fearless?" Maury said from the back seat of the truck. "You said you wet yourself when you heard the gunfire break out."

"That's just a defensive move. Classic bladder kung fu. Don't you know anything about women?"

"Apparently not," Maury said.

"All this has been as scary as a dentist with a jackhammer," Bonnie bubbled on, "but don't you know it feels good to have something knock me out of the rut of doing the same old, same old day after day? Life can blur into a string of bad television at home to soap opera days at work. I don't have any kids, and my ex only comes around when he's horny or been crying in his beer, or both. So I'm on board. You gotta stop at a drugstore, though, Al. I've

143

got to put together a new med kit if we're to keep Maury back there in top running form."

"Sure, put me in too, coach," Maury mumbled.

Bonnie said, "We should swing by your place real quick to go through your closets and cupboards, Al, and get him different clothes to wear. He's starting to look like someone they'd sweep outta the bus station for vagrancy."

Al grinned. "I admit I'm worried about you staying on board, Bonnie. But I'm glad you are. My spirits had been sinking. I've been stewing on Fergie, what we had just got going, and with life opening up, only to have to face the worst mess I've ever confronted. Which reminds me, I've got to call Fergie."

"I wish I'd gotten to you before that string bean."

"I appreciate the thought. But I'm spoken for."

"What about me?" Maury asked.

Bonnie turned to look back at him. "No offense, honey, but you're like an old car with five hundred thousand miles on it, and the license plate says, 'Hard-used horn-dog.'"

"Gee, why would I take offense to that?"

"There! There!" Bonnie pointed. "A drugstore."

Al swerved into the lot. "See if they have any clothes in there that might fit Maury. I don't think going to my place is a very good idea just now." He pulled out his credit card—one of the items to weather his wallet's dip into the lake better than most—and handed it to her. Signing his name on the little plastic credit card scanner screen would be a breeze for someone of her ingenuity.

She climbed out and hustled across the tarmac to go inside the store. Maury sat as still as a dozen tired mice in the back, so Al took out his cell phone, which he'd had the foresight to put in the plastic bag with the guns, and punched Fergie's number. The phone rang three times, then switched over to her answering service. He hung up without leaving a message.

"You know," Al said, "I've been trying to remember what it was like to fall in love."

"Do you think you're in love with Fergie?" Maury asked.

"I think so. I believe I am. As much as I can understand what that is anymore."

"You don't sound all that convinced to me. What are the symptoms, Einstein?"

"Well, there are a lot of things."

"You're going to have to be more specific."

"Have you ever been in love, Maury?"

"I don't want to talk about it."

"Aw, come on." Al glanced into the rearview mirror. Maury was sitting out of its range.

"I mean we probably shouldn't."

"Why? How many times?"

"Just the once."

"Come on. What was she, hideous or something?"

"No. Leave it alone."

"You know me. I'm not going to leave you alone until—"

"It was Abbie."

The quiet in the truck felt heavier, more profound. It stretched on and on. Maybe that was what Maury had been seeking all these years, that feeling again. Hell, it was what Al had probably been seeking himself without knowing it.

CHAPTER SEVENTEEN

A TRICKLE OF SWEAT RAN DOWN from Osiel's temple to his open shirt collar, even though he stood in the mottled shadows beneath a sycamore tree. The air felt hot and fetid and smelled of dust and baked brown grass. The breeze was hardly a breeze at all, a mere wistfulness. A creek bed ran through the copse of trees, but it had dried to just a few puddles that held water skippers on top and tiny minnows that darted among the mossy rocks. Mosquitoes circled his pant legs. He swatted one that landed on his sweaty forearm as he closed and pocketed the TracFone, still warm from holding it to his ear. He clambered up the slope and into the sunlit field, mowed of its hay some time ago, and followed its edge until he heard the *thump, thump, thump* of Flavio throwing. He couldn't see buildings in any direction he looked, which was why he'd picked the spot—and it was close enough to a tower to get reception. The first place he'd picked had been too far out.

The three of them had stayed in the shade nearest the camo tarp. Osiel gave the sleeping form of Donall Garcia a nudge with his toe as he went past. Donall stirred and took his ball cap off his face. Osiel held up a forefinger and swirled it in a couple of circles. That got the pilot scrambling to his feet.

Donall tugged on his cap as he went over to the thin

camouflage tarp. He started pulling it off, revealing the black McDonnell Douglas 500D helicopter that sat in the open, ready to take off. He'd gone on and on to Osiel about wishing he could get his hands on the much faster Sikorsky X2, but that was still in prototype. Besides, Osiel could fly the MD 500 in a pinch.

Eduardo sat on the ground with his back to the wide trunk of a pecan tree. He had a loaf of white bread open and a slice lying on each thigh. A slice of bologna and Monterey Jack cheese waited on one side. He was laying pickled jalapeño pieces onto a layer of mayonnaise on one of the slices. He looked up. "*Vamanos?*"

Osiel nodded.

Eduardo closed the sandwich, folded and pocketed his knife, and struggled to his feet, no easy task for someone close to three hundred pounds. He left the open jars of mayonnaise and jalapeños on the ground beside the loaf of bread and open packs of cheese and bologna. He rolled up the sandwich, gave it a squeeze, put one end in his mouth, and rushed to help Donall with the tarp.

Flavio was pulling his three throwing knives from the barkless trunk of a long-dead mesquite tree. He'd carved a heart chest-high, and every knife had been stuck inside the shape. When throwing, he went into a zone, so focused it was best not to go up on him quickly. Osiel made sure he rustled the leaf litter with his boots as he walked over to him. Flavio had been looking down at the points, feeling the knife edges.

When Flavio raised his head at the sound, Osiel again made the circling motion with his finger and tilted his head in the direction of the copter. He could hear its *whop, whop, whop* as the engine caught and began to warm up.

Flavio glared at him, eyebrows tightening, corners of his mouth pulled down hard.

"Hey," Osiel said. "Maybe this time I don't make you throw the heads overboard. Okay?"

Flavio's frown cracked, his face breaking into a grin of raw evil. Flavio nodded and started putting his knives into the three-slot scabbard strapped to his right thigh. Osiel and he had had long discussions about the merit of a bullet over a knife, but Flavio said the knife was more fun, more satisfying. Something sexual there, but Osiel hadn't pried. And he would never again get Flavio started on steel. The man's eyes took on a silvery hue when he spoke of S60V over, say, ATS-34, and he laughed aloud at 440C. Those were all different kinds of throwing knives, but Flavio might as well have been discussing the moons of Jupiter as far as Osiel cared. He'd handled Flavio's double-edged throwing knives before—custom built, each thirteen and a half inches long and five sixteenths of an inch thick, all one piece and as well balanced as any Osiel had ever seen.

When Flavio threw, it was nothing like what people might expect in a movie or circus performance. No snap of the wrist, nothing fancy. The sliver of steel seemed to shoot from Flavio's extended hand as he followed through, releasing on target with astounding accuracy. One minute in his hand, the next quivering in a tree, or a person. A machete hung in a sheath along his left thigh. He had used that often enough, too. Maybe too often.

Osiel was glad, though, when Flavio picked up the AK-47 he had leaned against a juniper. That was something Osiel could count on, good from any distance, and they had plenty of ammo.

Osiel led the way. Ahead, he could see Eduardo, all hulking muscle, climbing into the cabin. He was probably looking forward to breaking a neck or tearing out a liver. "We *are* the locos, the crazies," Osiel muttered. "No mistake about that." He grinned. That was the reason they always had work. None of them knew the meaning of the word "quit."

At the helicopter, Flavio climbed into the back and sat next to Eduardo, who was chewing the last bite of his sandwich.

Osiel got into the front passenger seat and fastened his seat belt. He waved at Donall and said, "*Pronto!*"

Donall nodded and nudged the throttle. The chopper rose into the air, and Osiel watched the land below go whizzing by—ranches, cattle, goats, wide stretches of browning grass, more hills than he expected, and a few limestone cliff faces. The houses began to cluster closer and closer together, then the highways filled with trucks of all sizes and cars, everybody going somewhere. The few people he saw were too tiny for him to tell if they were looking up. It didn't matter if they did. Soon they would be done. Very soon, he hoped.

Bonnie came bustling out of the drugstore with enough bags that Al knew next month's credit card bill was going to sting. Of course, after what had happened to the houseboat he'd rented, the handyman hired to fix the damage to his house, and the impending bill from Pinky, the drugstore purchases mattered very little in the scheme of things.

Once back in the passenger seat, Bonnie pulled out a burnt-orange T-shirt with Texas Longhorns across the front and XXXL below that.

"Oh, my lord," Maury muttered, and not just because he was going to look small, small, small in it. It was the kind of shirt he would never have bought.

Al's cell rang, and after glancing at the screen, he answered while opening his door. "Fergie! There you are.

I have an enormous favor to ask. No, not that, but we can—"

Bonnie said, "My guess is she keeps the phone on vibrate and has you call every few minutes." She climbed into the passenger seat and shut her door.

Al stepped outside and walked a few steps from the truck to finish the call in private. He asked his favor, and Fergie agreed. Two minutes later, Al popped back into the truck. He buckled his seat belt as he backed out of the parking spot.

"Whoa there, Trigger. Do you smell the barn?" Bonnie asked.

"He's had a whiff of something," Maury said.

Al glanced into the rearview mirror and saw Maury rolling his eyes. "Envy doesn't become you."

Al turned onto an elevated stretch of 183 that would carry them up through the city and eventually to the northern outskirts of Austin. Reds, yellows, and blues of businesses crowded close below them on either side—auto parts stores, groceries, and tattoo parlors.

"Ah, the scenic route," Maury said. "There're some pre-owned cars just waiting for pre-owned wives."

Bonnie turned in her seat. "Hey, no one ever owned me. But unless a tattoo has been removed from a certain delicate place, there's an ex out there someplace still wearing my brand."

Maury chuckled. "Ah, Bonnie. It's good to know that romance isn't dead—perhaps blind and lame, but still kicking."

They wove out onto smaller and smaller roads that led into the woods up a narrow, weaving two-lane road far outside the city limits. The mountain cedars and live oak trees were still green, but the tall bending grass varied from yellow to brown. As they passed over the tops of the higher hills, Al could look across expanses of the landscape and see the toll the drought was taking. The sycamores were browning early, and even some of the hardy cedars were dying and fading to orangey rust. The roll of wooded hills that should have been a solid green had taken on a sickly sunbaked hue.

Al had preferred his job out in the county over doing the same sort of thing in the city. Not that the citizens were nobler or tamer—probably the opposite if he took a close look. But he liked the feel of rolling through the county, passing lakes and seeing houses off by themselves, up on hills or way back long lanes, with windmills, knots of prickly pear cactus, horse pastures, and big trees with flat bottoms, nibbled that way by goats or cattle eating as high up as they could reach. He turned into a lane lined on either side by a three-strand barbed-wire fence.

"The safe house is way out here?" Bonnie asked.

"Not exactly."

Maury slid forward to poke his head between the two front seats. "Where the heck are we?"

Al steered around a final bend. As they passed a low stand of mesquite, the view opened up again to a yellowed field of grass that led up to a house. On its porch, which ran all the way across the front of the house, stood Fergie, looking to Al like the centerfold pinup to the *Kama Sutra*. She smiled and waved.

"This isn't the safe house," Maury said.

Al shook his head. "Nope. I have a hunch Jaime's safe house isn't going to prove to be very safe. You'll both be better off here."

Bonnie reached to grasp his forearm. "You're staying too, aren't you, Al?"

"No. Someone has to be at the safe house. Fergie has agreed to put you two up and watch over you here."

"So you end up the hero then. Right?" Maury said.

"Or dead." Al turned to look at Maury. "Don't go into a lot of crap about sacrifice and heroism. There's nothing like that attached to this at all. I've thought it all out, and this is the safest for you and Bonnie. I'm trained in law enforcement and have the best chances if things get ugly."

"That's just the sort of thing someone heroic would say." Bonnie's fingers tightened on his arm. "Don't go at all. Stay here with us."

"Someone has to go, Bonnie, and it might as well be me." He rolled to a stop in front of the house.

Fergie came off the porch and ran toward them. "Hey, come on inside, all. I picked up a couple of rotisserie chickens and made a big salad." Her eyes swept over the wrinkled, worn, and fishy-smelling clothes Bonnie and Maury wore as they climbed out of the truck. She ended on Al, who had caught a glimpse of his own tired, red-rimmed eyes in the rearview mirror and the raspy salt and pepper growth on his chin. "After we eat, you can all take the showers I can only imagine you've been craving."

"I think I'm going to try and see if I can eat chicken in the shower," Maury said. He took off toward Fergie's house at a surprising pace, given all he'd been through. "A shower. Think of it."

"Al says he's not going to stay with us here. Try to talk him out of that," Bonnie said then turned to catch up with Maury. Her drugstore bags flopped along at her sides as she passed him.

Maury paused and turned around. The eager glitter in his eyes at the prospect of a shower faded. He came back toward Al's truck, not dragging his feet but showing some of the exhaustion and wear from all he had been through. At first, his shoulders slumped, but he straightened them as he came up to Al's window. "Look, I'll go. You stay."

Al's eyes flicked to Fergie's. Hers got wider, and her head tilted to the right, a nod of sorts.

Al turned back to Maury. His brother looked both as tired as Al had seen him in a spell, and as intent. "I'm the one who has to do that."

"I'm the big brother, and they probably prefer me."

"Maybe. But I've still got some juice left in me, and if it comes to shooting, I know guns."

"I could learn."

"I'll bet you could. From Bonnie? It'd only take a week or two."

Fergie's eyes followed them back and forth, switching from one to the other.

"Maybe next time," Al said. "Get some rest. We may need you full of pep before this is over."

Maury hesitated. "Okay. If I get a chance, though, I'll show you I can be there for you for a change, instead of the other way around."

"Fine with me. Get cleaned up and rested for now."

"You're tired too. Shouldn't you come inside and do the same?"

"Wish I could. Hey, I think I hear a shower and some chicken calling you. Better hustle, or Bonnie might not leave any for you."

"Oh, cripes." Maury spun and started off toward the house again at what amounted to a near trot for him. He called back over his shoulder, "I mean it. I will go with you or instead of you."

"Just eat your chicken."

Maury picked up his pace and didn't look back this time.

Fergie smiled. "That was nice of you. Maury has no business being around the likes of those you'll be with, but it was good of him to offer."

153

Al nodded. His own head felt slow and tired, a little fuzzy. "Maybe we're learning how to be brothers again. Takes some practice and getting used to, I'm finding out."

Fergie stepped close to the truck and leaned against his door. She bent a little through the open window, and they kissed.

"Does that go any ways toward convincing you to stay?" she asked.

"Oh, lordy, I wish I could. But this mess is about to untangle, or unravel, and I've got to be there. Jaime Avila is expecting me. Actually, he's expecting Maury, too. But cheese is cheese."

"I'm glad you're not going into this blind, Al. Be ready for anything."

He nodded toward the glove box, where he'd put his two pistols, about the only things he'd been able to salvage from what he'd taken to the houseboat, which had become a federal crime scene. Her eyes grew sad, and that punched him somewhere just above the heart.

She leaned closer. The skin over her high cheekbones was taut and smooth. He looked deeper into the violet of her eyes. On into the black of her pupils, he saw the threads of all their past and a bit of the present they'd shared. He, as a nervous young boy again, had stared at her bare shoulder and the tiny strap where he was to pin the corsage, and his hands had shook as he just handed the flower to her. All the years reeled by, times he'd thought of her, bumped into her, times he'd not thought of her then run into her again. Every second and touch of their night together came back in Blu-ray close-up detail—the quiver of her flesh as she vibrated to the close of a second then a third orgasm. Her rising from the bed. Him watching her glide across the room. Did she jog? Oh, my lord, those legs. He'd thought of her while he was on the houseboat and in the cave, Bonnie squirming back against him, Maury's bony body on his other side. As he faded back into a dissolve to the present, he felt a feather of wistfulness flutter to the ground.

"You know, there's something I wanted to say to you." His words came out raspy. He cleared his throat.

"Stop right now. You're not going to do anything crazy, are you?"

"If you mean propose or go into detail about my feelings, no. I'm probably headed for crazy, but that's not it."

"Okay then."

"I guess we understand each other."

She put a hand on his arm, and the heat radiated all the way through him. "I'll call Walsh to come over and help watch the house."

"That should be perfect." He turned the key.

She stepped away from the truck, and he pulled away. He watched her fade to a tiny stick figure in his rearview mirror. Then he put the pedal down and drove faster.

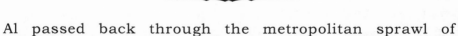

Al passed back through the metropolitan sprawl of Austin. Riding high atop an overpass and heading toward the safe house, he saw some of the same businesses he'd seen when they were going the other way. But he wasn't picturing families going to their favorite Sea Dragon Vietnamese-Chinese restaurant or cars filling the lots of movie theaters. Instead, he thought of the shady alleys where a hand holding money did a quick shake and slide-away from a hand holding a tiny plastic bag. He felt that he had seen more of the underside of life's rock than he ever had before. He could envision the nighttime network of drugs being sold everywhere, money pouring in, the escalation of Mexican Mafias, the turf wars between the

Zetas, the Mexikanemi, the Mara Salvatrucha, and battles between and among them and other cartels—all scrapping for turf in the big land of opportunity. It was like a dozen overturned anthills.

Hell, the druggies had their spots out in the county too—meth labs springing up like demented evil mushrooms in shacks, cabins, and, oh yes, the trailer courts. Al had been to his share of those delightful spots. But since the Combat Meth Act had made it so ephedrine and pseudoephedrine products could no longer be sold over the counter, the shift had swung in favor of the Mexican cartels and gangs wanting to do a little entrepreneurship. The normal flow of drugs of all kinds—heroin, cocaine, crack, marijuana, and methamphetamine—into cities like Austin had come about because of the increasing efficiency of cartels and gangs doing what they did in a businesslike way, yet with a ruthlessness beyond anything seen in corporate America and with more money at stake on the table. Teens and pre-teens were being recruited to be a part of it. If one fell, three sprang to take his place.

Al had been part of a task force to nab a marijuana load passing through where a fourteen-year-old and fifteen-year-old were part of the armed guard. Each had been paid four hundred dollars for the trip, and no one came to bail them out once they'd been locked up. Hell, a fourteen-year-old U.S. citizen from San Diego, working for the Beltrán Leyva brothers' drug cartel, had admitted to killing four people. He'd hung their beheaded bodies from a bridge in the tourist town of Cuernavaca. Yet he'd been sentenced to only three years in prison for organized crime, homicide, kidnapping, and drug and weapons possession, the maximum sentence allowed for a minor in that Mexican state, Morelos—another plus to the cartel people using minors.

A police raid of one Austin Zetas cell had turned up body armor, assault rifles, handguns, thousands in cash, and black-tar heroin. But it wasn't the goods as much as the particular kind of men. Los Zetas had started out as an offshoot of the elite Mexican military trained in Special Forces operations, next serving as hit men for the Gulf Cartel. They went on their own as a mercenary group comprised of members ranging from corrupt Mexican Federales, to politicians, to drug traffickers, and were said to be the most violent paramilitary group by the DEA.

In Mexico, there'd been a clash on the outskirts of the rural town of Ruiz when a convoy of Zetas had been ambushed by Sinaloa cartel gunmen. The bodies of the twenty-eight men found dead were wearing fatigues, bulletproof vests, cartridge belts, helmets, and military commando boots. Along with high-caliber weapons, fourteen SUVs, two of those armored, the investigators found over a thousand bullet casings and a few unexploded grenades. Army soldiers who were helping out harvested six rifles, a handgun, two hand grenades, ninety-six ammunition clips, over two thousand rounds of ammunition of different calibers, fourteen vehicles of different models, sixteen bullet-proof vests, eight cartridge belts, three Kevlar-style helmets, twenty-seven camouflage uniforms, and twenty-three pairs of military boots.

Yeah, it was a war, and what Al had seen of it didn't look much different from what he'd seen in the live coverage of troops fighting in Afghanistan and Iraq when that was at its peak. Al had played his small part in one twenty-month investigation of a drug ring based in Sinaloa, Mexico. A bust of their people in the U.S., led by the DEA and aided by more than a hundred federal, state, local, and foreign law enforcement agencies had seized forty-five-million dollars' worth of drugs—twenty-seven thousand pounds of marijuana, almost ten thousand pounds of cocaine, seven hundred pounds of methamphetamine, two hundred pounds of pure methamphetamine, and eleven pounds of heroin.

So Al had to wonder why ICE was making such a fuss over what would be to them a tiny trickle of erectile dysfunction drugs. Perhaps it was a slim tentacle that was part of the bigger beast. It had to be bigger. Maybe the Zetas were trying to gouge out a rival's network like a bad eye, and with the U.S. as the war zone. For Jaime Avila, the case had become about a cop killing. As wars went, there was little in the way of honorable about it—courage, respect, sacrifice. Yet there was plenty of money for betrayal and corruption. That was what it was really about: drawing the line in the sand about who could be trusted and who could be bought.

The tipping point in all of it was Jaime. Al had known him for years as a man of passion, apparently not just on the job. But when it came to his job, Jaime's veins ran with pure ICE. Many law officers looked at the "Protect & Serve" of their role as a lot of puffy air intended to soothe the mainstream population. *To serve.* The very idea! Many pictured themselves as gunslinger fighters of evil, swaggering with large guns hung low on their hips. That might be the way of some lawmen, or even other members of ICE—certainly those two who'd gone down back in the houseboat—but to Jaime, it was a different war. He might be a general in it, but the fight wasn't about being a hero for him, but in waging a war against a growing cancer that took managing some pretty rough talent to fight back effectively. And the fight had just cost him two men.

To many of the others in ICE, Maury probably didn't matter one iota in all that, nor did Al. They were bits of gravel in the way of larger moving vehicles. Being involved could mean Al might die, not get to fade out in dirty underwear, old and alone. But he was showing up at the safe house because he trusted Jaime. He was part of Jaime's life, and Jaime was part of his. He was doing it because he was driven by his emotional links to others. When a man did things for others with no expectation of getting something in return, that was love—though that might also be why love was so often misguided, misunderstood, and likely as not, unappreciated. There had been times, alone in his house, when he had felt pretty unattached to anyone else in the world and had even hoped to be bounced out of his everyday rut. *Ha.* Now he cared about Maury again. He cared about Fergie, though he'd hate to be at the offtrack betting window placing a wager on the outcome of that. Hell, he even cared about perky and bouncy Bonnie. And the bigger question: would he still be doing this if they weren't at stake? Well, yes, because he was just that sort of dumbass. The sensation that he wasn't connected to the world at any one place began to ease.

He was so bone-ass tired he wasn't even sure if he trusted his own ability to think. He didn't know if what he was doing was really the best and only way to play the game. Maybe. At least he was the only one exposed to any real danger.

Thoughts kept going over and over in his head until they were a blur, bumping into each other, varied permutations run out to their ends on the chess board, again and again. Yet there was no accounting for the unexpected. All he had to work with was everything he knew so far.

He shook his head and made himself stop and change the subject. Maybe it was in the end just knowing who he really was, what he wanted, what he was willing to spend to get it. *Bah!*

For the rest of the way to the safe house, he thought

about Fergie, of the way touching her skin made her feel precious to him. He pondered the notion that, yes, he was glad she was back in his life. Did that mean his remaining days would be better if she stayed in it? Was she the one with whom he could gracefully grow older? He seemed to be trying to fall in love with her. How was he doing with that? Was he fooling himself? Or her him? He'd played that both ways before. Nothing came of speculating on it, so he reverted to just stewing about whether he was going to come out of this alive—part of that was trying to make sure the guy in the vehicle next to him, with his head down while he texted on his cell phone, didn't slide into him and knock him off the overpass.

Al eased his truck down a cross street and looked down the street he wanted as he passed it. In the middle of the block, the safe house with dark grey siding, was a two-story job standing between two other houses of similar design that varied only in color. A jet taking off from the nearby Austin-Bergstrom Airport passed overhead so close the rippling sheer of air pressed down and rattled his truck to its tires. The roar was deafening. Gee, it must be swell to live in that neighborhood. He guessed that was why the homes were so affordable. He went around to the other end of the block and peeked down the street from that direction. No pile-up of parked vehicles. That was good. A string of black SUVs would have been less good. He'd have pulled away, in that case.

He made one more loop to look behind the house. Along the back of the property, a six-foot cedar fence ran beside the alley. Across from that was a playground where a few cars had been parked in the gravel lot, a hearty walk away from the swing set where kids were swinging and sliding down slides.

He figured Jaime would have the houses on either

side of the safe house, too. That was how Al would do it. ICE had its own special reaction teams and SWAT units, so they'd be hidden but locked and loaded. The set-up seemed sort of safe, but things had a tendency to slip and slide. The Zetas were trained mercenaries, some of them with Special Forces backgrounds. Osiel Cárdenas Santiago almost certainly had been one, and Flavio, the knife expert, and Eduardo the gun and muscle, apparently enjoyed a hobby of torture as well. So Al wouldn't have bet heavy money on Jaime's plan. Al very well might be betting his own life. It made the butterflies in his stomach get butterflies in their stomachs.

When he got to the street again, he drove down it then turned into the house's driveway. Before he reached the end, the door to the two-car garage opened. One space was filled by a black SUV. No surprise there. He pulled his truck into the empty space, and the door began to close behind him. He took the Glock out of the glove box, slipped it inside his belt at the small of his back, and tugged his shirt out to hang over it.

Al got out of his truck, went to the door leading to the inside, opened it, and passed through a laundry room, then on through the kitchen into the living room. Jaime sat in one of two matching monkey-shit-brown recliners positioned across from an old-fashioned television with a converter box on top. A soccer game announcer rattled away in staccato Spanish. Sergio stood beside one of the two front windows. With one hand, he held up a slat of the closed Venetian blinds so he could peek out, and his other hand held the garage door remote.

"Where's that constipated gerbil of a brother of yours?" Jaime asked. He touched the remote on his lap, and the television went silent.

Al could hear the wind rasping against the house then

the growing roar of another plane that rattled the room like a maraca until it doppled upward and onward, out of range. "You don't need him. I can be the bait on your hook."

His lips tightened. "What if we wanted to talk with him?"

"I don't think he knows as much as you think he does."

"He knows enough." Jaime's voice got louder. He jumped to his feet and slammed the remote onto the recliner seat. "I trusted you, Al. You'd put this mission at risk? What do you think you're fucking with here, some nickel-dime operation? We've got—" He stopped mid-sentence and stood there like a slow burning ember in a fireplace.

Sergio stepped away from the window to glare at Al. "Yeah, what the hell, man? We risk everything and you..." It was hard for Sergio to shout through clenched teeth. Al could practically see the man internally throwing cold water on himself, dousing the fires of irritation. Sergio rolled his head around once, crackled loose some tension in his neck. "Where are they? Just tell us."

Al shook his head. "I don't have to tell you that."

Jaime let out an irritated puff of air. "I think it'd be a good idea, Al. Trust us." His voice had managed to relax as well, back to pure professionalism. "We may need to protect them before this is over. We can't very well work with you if this isn't a two-way street. We've both been to this rodeo before."

Al hesitated, looking deep into Jaime's brown eyes. They *had* worked together often, and well. But all the same, Jaime didn't do a two-way street. It was all one-way with him. Al held back.

Jaime lowered his head for a moment. Then he raised it, his eyes lit up. He nearly shouted, "They're at Fergie's place, aren't they?"

"Fergie?" Sergio asked.

"Detective Ferguson Jergens, a city cop. You know her."

"That's not—" Al started.

"Oh, no good you going out on a limb here. It's the only thing makes sense. We know she's been out to your place. We do know stuff, and we can figure the rest out. All I wanted to do was know where your brother is, just in case." Jaime tilted his head, relaxed and confident again. "Now, Al. You haven't succumbed to the allure of a woman in uniform, have you?" He grinned like a kid catching another with a hand in the candy jar.

"Detectives don't wear uniforms. And no."

"Still, you sound a touch defensive. Well, I'm glad there are still bullets in the old gun."

"It's not such an old gun."

"Aw, what the hell, Al. I'm sorry I blew up on you. We're still good. We're on. I had Sergio pick up some grub for you and your pals. Why don't you tuck in? Maybe take a shower and grab a nap. I think we have some daylight to burn yet." He turned to Sergio. "Why don't you show him to a room?"

Sergio nodded. He had reverted to his perpetual scowl, so Al got about as much out of him as he might sitting across a poker table from him. Sergio crossed the room, one careful foot in front of the other, gradually faster, as if going down a slight hill. John Wayne had walked the same way in almost every western.

Al followed Sergio into the kitchen, where three orange-striped Whataburger bags sat on the counter beside the sink. Al grabbed one of them. He debated picking up a second one, but Sergio was back on the move, so Al tagged along. They went up the stairs and down a hallway to a room at the end. Al pulled a couple of the fries out of the bag and popped them in his mouth. Cold but delicious. He tried to remember when he'd last eaten. Sergio stopped at the door and stood aside. Al opened the door, and went inside. Sergio stepped in afterward and took a quick look around the room before waving a dismissive limp-handed goodbye and leaving. Al closed the door.

The room had the sort of bedroom furniture that could be bought as a package without breaking the bank. The bedstead, dresser, and nightstand all matched—veneered cherry. Al opened the two other doors. One led to an empty walk-in closet, the other to a bathroom—not fancy but with a bar of soap in a wrapper and a clean towel, perhaps new, folded on the sink.

He went back and sat on the side of the bed. First things first. He devoured the cold cheeseburger and ate all the fries. He watched himself eat in the dresser mirror, and at any other time, he would have been embarrassed by his dining style—starved caveman gone piranha. Al was the kind of person who had watched people eat in restaurants and thought the best hell for someone like them would be to have to watch other people eat like themselves through eternity. Apparently, he had become one of their number.

He finished, wadded the bag into a lump, and took it into the bathroom where he'd seen a small trashcan. Then he turned down the bed, slid his gun out from the small of his back, and put it under the pillow. He tugged off his clothes, got into the shower, and let the water beat down on him for five minutes until he felt himself nodding off.

When he went back into the room, the closet door was still open, and he could see someone climbing backward down a wooden folding ladder that descended from the attic. Before Al could yell, someone very big grabbed him in an arm lock from behind and clamped a hand over his mouth. Al was shoved forward, causing his towel to drop. Naked, he fell face first on the bed. His assailant flipped him over onto his back and pressed his rough, calloused hand back over Al's mouth, hard. A tall man stood on the other side of the bed, holding a roll of silver duct tape and a double-edged knife with a long glittering blade.

"Be still," the big man who held him said with a heavy Latino accent.

Al flexed every tired muscle he had, trying to break free. The hands gripping him tightened, squeezing him harder, the man still just hinting while showing Al he had a whole lot more strength in reserve. He could break Al in half, but that might steal some of the knife guy's fun.

Al was amazed by the amount of detail he could gather when he thought the next few minutes would be his last. It wasn't as if he was going to need the information for a lineup or anything. Yet he was absorbing and storing away each last nanosecond of life.

Osiel Cárdenas Santiago, the cell leader stepping away from the ladder and coming to join the others, was shorter by far than the other two, but he had the prison-flinty look of someone old enough to have made all the mistakes he was ever going to make. Nor did he look patient or even a tiny bit tolerant. Beneath his thinning salt and pepper hair Al could make out the shadings of a complex tattoo, but the eyes that glittered in obsidian glee were what bothered Al.

Of Flavio, who leaned in to peer at Al as if he were a food selection at a cafeteria, Al seemed to see only the silvery flash of the knife. He knew the man was tall and had dark hair above a face shaped like an inverted pyramid with thin lips. The double-edged knife looked very sharp, as though it had been lovingly honed, often. Flavio kept turning it in his hand so it kept up its steady hypnotic glitter. Al spent most of his time staring at the turning, shining blade.

When he had been a young boy, Al had had his share of scaly nightmares, but none of them came close to the way the three men made his skin try hard to crawl itself inside out. Being held naked and shivering on the bed while waiting to be carved like a Thanksgiving turkey didn't help.

They seemed to be taking their time. No hurry, and why should there be with Jaime and the others downstairs peering out the windows and waiting, while Osiel and his crew were already inside. It puzzled Al that they didn't seem to want to ask him any questions, such as why Maury wasn't there or where his brother was.

Then the realization burst through that they already knew that somehow. He didn't know how they knew, but they did. He was just going to be a bit of sport before they moved on. For the barest flash of a second, he wondered what they would do with his head. Al would pay the price, then Maury, Fergie, and Bonnie. He'd failed them. Failed them miserably. He began to toss and surge against the arms holding him with everything he had.

Eduardo's thick brows bunched as he struggled to hold Al in place. The effort made his wide, round face scrunch up, like a baby about to cry. But he was strong enough to manage Al. His grin said that, in spite of the tussle, he was enjoying himself—never a good sign. His foul breath huffed in Al's face as he pressed closer, squeezed harder, all the while grinning that oafish evil grin.

In that brief flurry of activity, Al was thinking over his chances. None, really, the way he saw it. He saw Flavio tear off a strip of silver tape and lean forward, holding it sticky side out. The instant Eduardo took his hand off Al's mouth, Al screamed like an entire busload of seven-year-old girls.

He saw Eduardo's fist, the size of a pickup, whooshing toward his face, and the lights went out.

CHAPTER EIGHTEEN

A L'S EYES OPENED TO THE hammering that seemed, at first, to come from inside his own head. He forced his eyes open and, through the initially reluctant slits, saw Sergio over by the window standing close, face-to-face, with Osiel. Then Osiel turned and climbed out the open window, his face there for a second and as quickly gone.

Sergio turned his back to Eduardo, who hit him a chopping blow that dropped him. Eduardo climbed out the window and disappeared, too. Al sorted through the fading fog of coming to and felt more than a little surprised to find he was alive. He took deep gulping breaths and brought one hand up to touch his own neck, a natural enough response to knowing Flavio was probably the one of them with a fondness for cutting off the heads of their victims.

The door crashed open, and men in black SWAT gear poured into the room. They cleared the closet, attic, and bathroom. At the window, they shouted then shot bursts of automatic fire. The men dropped back as someone returned fire. Bullets shattered the window, throwing glass shards and splinters from the wooden frame across the room. Some pieces fell as far as where Al lay. One of the SWAT men stood over him, holding a Sig much like his own in both hands and fixed on him. The seconds stretched out, giving Al time to examine the gun in detail. He stared into the gaping barrel, which looked unusually large from his angle. Another man hovered over Sergio, who lay still on the floor.

Al listened to the shouting outside, still taking his time to make sense of all that had gone on and was still happening.

Only a few ticks later, a couple of the SWAT men raced back out the door, while others went through the window. They were on the second floor, so there must be a rope or some kind of ladder hanging down the side of the building. It was the only way he could make sense of it. His mind seemed slow to start. He sought to assemble details then realized he was naked. He wanted to reach for the covers to pull them over himself, but he looked into the unblinking eyes of the man in position over him and decided to lay still.

After what seemed a painfully long time for Al to be stared at under the circumstances, Jaime bustled into the room and made hand signs at the men in gear. The one hovering over Al lowered his weapon and joined the one standing over Sergio.

"Get your clothes on pronto, Al. We're going to have to hustle to catch up." Jaime went over to look out the window.

"They got away?" Al grabbed his clothes and sneakers, planning to get dressed in what was going to be a new record time for him.

"Of course they did. Worst springing of a finely tuned trap I've ever been a part of. Happens this way if they've gotten to one of your best men. Their edge is they always have tons of money, and I hope they had to dump one God awful lot of it to cause this."

The other two men lifted Sergio onto the bed. One took

out a pair of handcuffs. They rolled Sergio, who may well have been their immediate superior, onto his side. They pulled his arms back and put a set of cuffs on his wrists behind his back.

With Al fresh from the shower, his clothes felt dirty and mildly damp and smelled funky. But wearing them felt far better than being naked in front of all those men. He pulled them on as quickly as he could, tied his shoes tight, then reached under the pillow and pulled out his Glock. No one stopped him when he put it back in place at the small of his back.

Sergio's eyes were just opening when Jaime snapped, "Let's go."

The two men got Sergio to his feet. He blinked, struggled for a second or two, then looked across the room at Jaime.

"Yeah, the whole thing's on tape, Serg. I had orders to find and plug the leak. Now, let's go. Because of you, these guys are in the wind."

Sergio shrugged. He was a man who had taken chances and known the odds. As Jaime walked past, Sergio suddenly surged forward, looking as though he was trying to bite and kick at the same time. The two men yanked him backward and slammed him to the floor with a loud thud. He twisted, squirmed, and kicked. Jaime pointed at Sergio's feet, and the men put a strap around his ankles, too.

As Jaime watched, his expression galloped through disappointment and sadness then ended on anger. He hustled out of the room, and Al followed.

"I know the shortest way to Fergie's place," Al said. He'd had some food, a shower, and a short nap of sorts, though his head still throbbed as a consequence.

"I know a better one." Jaime accelerated his pace, taking the stairs two at a time.

They passed through the house and out the open front door. Jaime stopped at a row of three black SUVs and got into the backseat of the third one. This was looking more like an ICE operation.

Al climbed in after him then watched four men carry out Sergio, who had either settled down or had been sedated, and load him into the SUV ahead of them.

"I loved that man like a brother," Jaime said. "The son of a bitch." He spit toward the floor as their SUV pulled out behind the others.

The first two accelerated until they were out of sight on the way toward the highway. The one they were in pulled into the park behind the house. A couple of the men in black gear were keeping the mothers and children away from an open soccer field. The family groups huddled into a knot by the swing sets, either scared or fascinated at seeing something more real than they'd ever seen on television. Al heard the copter approaching as the SUV stopped in a spray of sliding gravel. Jaime popped open his door and took off in a vigorous jog.

If it had been the sheriff's department springing to action, Al knew there would have been a lot of double-checking, communications, and being careful. Not so with ICE. They took off with daring energy, like a loose handful of rockets. Had it been any other situation, Al might have preferred the more ploddish care of the department ways. But they were working to keep Osiel from his commitment to take out Maury and whoever happened to be near him. Al figured he could do things Jaime's way this once.

Al climbed out of the vehicle and tagged along behind Jaime, having to step lively to keep up with the other man's pace. The heat of the day slammed down, the sun beaming from the relentless blue of a cloudless sky. He was glad when Jaime slowed, then stopped in the soccer field, within a dash of the open landing area.

Al caught up, breathing hard. He'd seen Jaime's dismount before and suspected his climb into the craft would be just as abbreviated. There was no time for the tiredness he'd felt earlier to register. Adrenalin was surging through him in throbbing waves. That made him think of Fergie's brother, back home from the war and unable to savor the calm of a peaceful environment.

The helicopter came into sight—the same one as before, from the look of it. It lowered to the ground, hammering the grass flat with its blades. The craft had barely settled into a light bounce before Jaime was off and running. Al panted along behind, glad he still wore the sneakers that'd been through quite a day or two. The shoes were holding up better than he was. If he made it through all this, perhaps he ought to go back to taking light daily jogs. Those were the days—good breakfast and a trot through the cooler air of the mornings. He took the extended hand of what looked to be the door gunner and hopped inside to take a seat next to Jaime.

Jaime fastened his seatbelt and said, "Take it up, Cody."

Cody turned out to be the fellow who had helped Al inside. He had closely buzzed hair and the face of an eighteen-year-old but the body of a weight-lifter. He wore his Sig in a holster that hung halfway down his right thigh and was tied around his leg with a leather strap at the lower end.

Al had barely plopped into his seat before the chopper jerked into its lift. He grabbed the end of the seatbelt and snapped it into place as the copter tilted in a turn and was off. The little upturned faces below grew smaller, then faded out of sight, replaced by the green tops of

171

the canopies of trees and the multi-colored rooftops of residential then patches of business buildings below.

Jaime held his cell phone tight to his ear, yelling and shaking his head. He hung up and leaned toward Al. Over the roar of the whopping roar of the engine, he yelled, "Figures. They had a helo ready, too. Got a good jump on us."

Jaime signaled to Cody for more speed, and the engine got louder. He opened his phone again and started dialing. "Calling Clayton!"

Though he shouted, Al could barely make out what he said.

A minute later, Jaime closed his phone and leaned closer again. "Sheriff's on the other side of the county. He's coming, but it'll be a while."

Fergie tilted her head, ear up, from where she was putting the dishes from their lunch into the dishwasher. The hum grew louder as it got closer, until it was an approaching *whop, whop, whop* of a roar. She'd heard a lot of helicopters in her day but didn't recognize the aggressive sound of this one. Perhaps she imagined a sense of menace in it. Something was there, though, enough to make her stop what she was doing.

As she walked fast through the living room, Maury shot up from the sofa. Bonnie, who had been coming down the stairs, still dabbing and rubbing at her hair with a towel after her shower, followed her to the front door.

Fergie pushed it open. Halfway up the drive and coming fast she saw a blue and white pickup truck she knew well. "That'll be Walsh. He said he was on his way." Fergie glanced up at the sky. The black copter was just coming into clear sight.

"What's that? STAR flight?" Maury asked.

Fergie shook her head. "That's no damn STAR flight."

"Is it Al's friend Jaime?" Bonnie said.

"Nope. Not him either." Fergie squinted as she looked up into the bright sky.

"Fast, isn't it?" Maury said.

"Oh. Oh. Uh oh." Fergie grabbed for Maury and Bonnie. "You guys better—"

Before she could finish, the helicopter caught up to the approaching two-tone truck. First, Fergie heard the *chop, chop, chop* of carefully spaced shots from an automatic weapon. A line of smoke whooshed out of the side of the chopper and slammed into the drive just ahead of the truck, exploding and gouging a huge hole in the drive. The truck swerved to go around the hole.

"Led him too much," Fergie said before she could stop herself. She glanced toward Bonnie, whose mouth hung open.

The truck was still coming. A second later, it exploded. The doors flew off in two directions, and the front rose in a lurch that nearly tossed the vehicle over backward. Not that it mattered. The engine burst into flames that swept into the dried brown grass around it.

Fergie swallowed. "You guys. Come here quick."

"You okay?" Bonnie said.

Fergie wiped her face, feeling the wet on her cheeks. "Yeah. I'm fine." She fought past a catch in her throat. "Let's move." She closed the door and locked it, though she doubted that would matter.

Fergie shot across the living room to her gun safe, Bonnie and Maury rushing to keep up. She hurried to spin through the combination and screwed up in her first try. Fingers shaking, she got it on the second attempt and popped open the door. She grabbed her automatic

173

shotgun, made sure the safety was off, and handed it to Maury. "You okay with that?"

He raised his gaze from the gun in his hands and looked her in the eyes. "Yeah, sure. But I'm gonna need plenty of ammo."

He surprised her. No foot-dragging. No reluctance. It was all she could ask for. She waved a hand toward rows of boxes of ammo along the bottom of the safe. All the shotgun shells were twelve gauges, so no chance for confusion there. She bent to grab an unopened box of .30-.06 ammo. She took out the appropriate rifle with scope. She didn't have to wonder about Bonnie, who had gone country-girl squinty-eyed, ready to shoot anything.

"What's your preference?" Fergie said.

Bonnie bent to grab a box of .38 Special hollow-point ammo and pulled the small Chiefs Special out of the ankle holster that hung on the right wall of the safe.

"You sure?" Fergie asked her.

"I'll be fine. Back door?"

"Great. Maury, can you watch the front?"

When he nodded, Fergie went to the closet next to the gun safe, yanked it open, and pushed aside her uniform jackets, flak jackets, bulletproof vests, and rain gear to grab her favorite brown hunting jacket. She slipped it on and walked back to the gun safe. She hesitated then added a box of shotgun shells to her pile and pulled out the Winchester Model 12. *What the hell. Might as well pull out the stops.*

She clutched the rifle and shotgun in one hand, the boxes of ammo in the other, and ran up the stairs to the second floor. In the spare bedroom, she propped the shotgun next to the window, raised the glass, and looked outside. She couldn't see the front drive, so she rushed across the upstairs to a window on the other side and yanked that one open. She saw the ball of flame that had once been Walsh's truck.

She knelt, brought the rifle to her shoulder, and focused the scope on the truck, but she couldn't see Walsh's body. Fergie caught a black blur in the upper corner of the scope and raised the barrel. The copter was turning, picking up speed, and coming right toward the house. She refocused, fixed on the middle of the windshield, and fired, worked the bolt and pulled the trigger again. The helicopter tilted into a sudden lift and shot up out of her line of sight. She lowered the rifle when she heard the chopper going around to the other side of the house.

She got to her feet and ran across the upper floor to look out that window. The helicopter was squaring up so its open side door was toward the house.

Bam! Bam! The shots came from downstairs.

"Oh, Bonnie, you'll never hurt a copter with that little gun." But Fergie heard a *ka-ching* as a shot ricocheted off the side of the chopper.

The driver must have jerked the controls because the craft snapped a little to the left. By the time he'd steadied it, Fergie had her rifle up. With no time to aim with the scope, she fired, worked the bolt, and fired again. The copter tilted and whooshed out of range again. She doubted she'd hit anything, but it sure felt good to see the damned thing back off.

"Hey!" Maury yelled from downstairs. "You're not going to believe this."

"What?" Fergie yelled. She pulled out the clip and began reloading the rifle.

"It's Walsh."

She propped the rifle on the other side of the window from the shotgun, spun, and ran to hurry down the stairs. When she hit the bottom floor, Maury was looking out the open front door. Fergie spotted Walsh in front of the gun safe. He reached for the .308 next to the muzzleloader.

"Walsh? I can't believe it," she said. "You're alive?"

He turned to grin at her. "Either that or I'm one pissed-off ghost. Fuckers just blew up my truck. Only had two more payments."

She rushed over and hugged him. "Wish there was more time to chat."

"Gotcha. Where can you use me?" He bent to get a box of .308 ammo.

"Upstairs. I'll be right up there with you. I want to have a word with Maury and Bonnie first." She grabbed her service piece from the safe and a couple of boxes of 9mm ammo.

Walsh nodded and hurried up the stairs.

"Bonnie!" Fergie yelled.

"Yeah?"

"Come 'ere. I want us to have a short huddle."

<hr />

Al and Jaime sat in silence, except for the droning whop of the blades that vibrated all the way through Al's tired bones. He was doing the math on how long it would take Clayton to come help. Jaime's men too, for that matter.

Jaime leaned closer, but still had to shout. "When it's your partner, even a past one, you don't always respond the way you might if it was anyone else. You've had each other's back too many times to count, lost track of how many times you've saved each other's life. I could always count on Sergio. Dammit! Dammit! Dammit! I gave him every chance, even when it came to exposing himself as the leak. I knew he had some money troubles, his own damn fault, but I thought he'd sort it out without going this direction."

Al nearly added that giving Sergio that slack had cost a couple of men, as well as given away Maury's location, but Jaime's twisted, anguished expression encouraged him to say nothing. Jaime already knew. He probably also knew that the reason he wanted to get the Zetas cell so much was all tied up in that, too. Al hoped that didn't make Jaime careless.

More rooftops zipped by below then tops of trees, waves of green, yellow, and orange climbing one tired, sun-burned hill after another. Al leaned back in his seat and tried to relax to store energy for what was coming ahead.

Jaime pointed at Al's pocket. "Maybe you'd better call."

Al nodded, took out his cell phone, and dialed.

After two rings, Fergie answered, "Kinda busy here."

He could hear the sounds of shots in the background. "Can you hold them off? We're en route."

"Roger." With a little more emotion, she added, "Hurry."

Al hung up and looked out the window. He recognized a few features of the land below and could tell they were getting closer. He saw a string of three sheriff's department cruisers with red and blue lights flashing, heading the same direction, but his quick calculation had them too far from Fergie's house to be there in less than fifteen or twenty minutes. The ICE copter left them behind—too far behind, Al thought—and their flickering lights soon faded from his sight. A few miles later, the chopper peeled off from the road they'd been following and started up Fergie's lane. He spotted the house. Another helicopter sat on the other end of the field behind the house just before that turned into woods.

"Cody!" Jaime yelled.

The pilot nodded. "I see it."

The helicopter pitched in a sharp turn then jerked back the other way, tossing Al from left to right. When he could glimpse the ground again for a second, he saw a man, probably Eduardo from the bulk, standing not far from the other chopper. He had a tube on his shoulder, and he was pointing it up at them.

"*Madre dios!*" Jaime made the sign of the cross. In one hand, he held the silver crucifix he had tugged from beneath his shirt—not a reassuring sight for Al.

Cody kept up his evasive maneuvers, zigzagging as the engine roared at its loudest as he sought to get them out of range. Al, who had seen such tubes, unbuckled his seat belt, got out his pistol from behind his back, and slid it deep into his pocket.

Al felt the round slam into the chopper. He expected an explosion. The copter tilted sideways, and Cody fought a losing battle with the controls. They started down. The blades began to cut into treetops, and the engine stuttered. Al could see a rush of green going by a few yards below.

The instant they were a few feet closer Al shot up out of his seat, looked for the biggest clump of green, and leaped out the side door. He had skydived before, but he'd had a parachute. The air rushed at him, the green canopy of treetops seeming to grow brighter, clearer. From the corner of his eye, he saw the helicopter crash sideways into the trees in a roar of rending blades and screeching metal. Next came a dull boom and the flash of an orange ball of flame.

Al smashed into the top branches and immediately grabbed at any he could reach. The tiny branches snapped beneath his clutching fingers, and leaves ran through his fingers. He bounced off one slightly larger limb, knocking some of the wind out of him. But the impact slowed him enough that he was able to a good hold on the next bigger limb. That branch broke, and he fell again.

He grabbed and managed to grasp a bigger limb. That

one bent, then snapped him up again before dropping him onto another limb. He wrapped his arms around the branch as tightly as his tired body would allow and hung there for a few seconds until he could breathe normally.

He pulled himself hand-over-hand toward the trunk. Once there, he got his feet on a second limb and rested a few more ticks. He heard the rumble of another explosion. *Oh, great. Just what these tinder-dry woods need.* Al tried not to think of Jaime and Cody, but it was the same old "try not to think of a white bear" all over again. He saw both of their faces clearly in his mind, even though he'd only just met Cody.

He tried to tell himself they had survived, that they were okay too. He had made it, after all. But he knew when he was selling a lie.

Al started downward as fast as he could safely go. The sense of urgency pounding at him took him past the aches and pains throughout his entire body. He heard shots—some rifle or pistol, others the bigger boom of a shotgun—punctuated by the response of bursts from an automatic weapon.

He slid down the last stretch of trunk right into an Agarita bush, which looked like holly but with hard leaves that had razor edges. *Fine. Just fine.* He tumbled out of that and stood up. A couple of ribs felt cracked, his left wrist felt sprained, and he was covered in cuts and bruises. Blood trickled down across his right temple from his scalp. But he was alive.

He looked toward where the copter had crashed. He could hear the crackle of flames. At least the breeze was blowing away from the house, for now. That might not matter for long.

He took out his cell phone to call 9-1-1, but the screen was obscured by a spider-webbed crack, and the keypad didn't respond to his touch. He shoved it back into his pocket, pulled out his gun, got his bearings, and began to limp toward the house. Apparently, his left ankle had gotten sprained as well. *Great.* He limped faster.

The trees in front of him thinned enough for him to catch glimpses of the house. Sporadic gunfire helped keep him on track. He half dragged his left leg, trying to run, but falling a good ways short of that. He spotted Eduardo ahead and to the right. The man still held the rocket launcher, this time aimed toward the house.

A few feet ahead, some limestone rocks had been loosely piled from where they'd been cleared from the fields. The long chest-high row was sprinkled with prickly pear cactus. The obstacle ran too far in both directions for Al to get around them quickly. The only way was straight over.

He charged the heap and tried to land his feet on the stones. When he missed, the green oval cactus heads with their long spines scraped his legs, sometimes piercing his flesh and even going through his sneakers. No time to pause, though. It was like running through a bed of coals. He kept his eyes on the other side and at last made it through the last of the rocks and cacti, out into open tall yellow-brown grass, which was all bent to one side.

"Hey!" he yelled. *"Basta! Pendejo!"* He didn't have as much Spanish as he should for a former lawman in Texas, and he'd just used up most of it.

Eduardo kept the rocket launcher aimed toward the house.

Al raised his gun and squeezed the trigger. The bullet hit the metal tube of the launcher, ricocheted off with a clang, and went into the side of Eduardo's neck. The end of the launcher lowered then fell toward the ground, hanging by its strap.

The big man turned slowly and tried to reach for one of

the pistols in his belt. Before he could draw, he fell over onto his face and lay still.

Al thought about stopping and gathering Eduardo's weapons but instead took off at what passed for a run in his condition. A crippled snail might have overtaken him. But he grew closer to the house with each dragged step.

When he was about fifty feet from the house, a tall thin man popped up from behind what used to be Fergie's car— now a bullet-riddled hulk with flat tires. Flavio pointed an AK47 right at Al's gut and clicked on an empty chamber. Flavio popped out the spent clip and started to reach for another, then he seemed to remember his knives, and he moved his hand toward the scabbard on his right hip.

A shotgun blast from the house shattered the car's windshield, throwing a spray of crystal bits of safety glass across him. Flavio had one arm almost to his knife quiver, but before he could grab and throw the knife a second shot blasted out the driver's side window. He ducked behind the far side of the car.

Al scrambled to his feet and headed for the house at a limping gallop. Maury lowered his shotgun and stepped to one side. Maury looked as fit and full of vinegar as Al had seen him in some time. *Good to see him coming around.* Al leaped up onto the porch, dove through the window, and rolled, just as a pistol shot chipped off a piece of the wooden window frame. Flavio had just remembered he carried a sidearm.

Al slid to a stop on his back, gasping. The second he had half a lungful of air again, he huffed, "Was in the area. Thought I'd drop in."

CHAPTER NINETEEN

MAURY HAD THREE BOXES OF twelve-gauge shells open, and he was shoving shells into a Remington automatic shotgun. He watched out the window for any movement behind what had once been Fergie's car. He wore the XXXL burnt orange Longhorns shirt over grey sweat pants, along with Al's back-up sneakers. He wasn't going to win any *GQ* prizes, though he looked comfortable enough. The shirt made him appear bulked up, as if he'd gained twenty or thirty pounds—though he wasn't quite up to football lineman yet. The arms that hung out of the huge sleeves still looked no bigger around than knitting needles.

"Amazing gadgets, these." Maury held up the shotgun. "Who'd have thought I'd ever know how one worked, much less be using it?"

"Not me." Al got gingerly to his feet, every part of him aching and throbbing. He put his pistol inside his belt at the front. "How're we fixed for ammo?"

"I think Fergie has the kind for your gun upstairs."

"Great. I'd better get some. You and I can catch up later."

"Fine. I'll have my people call your people." Maury winked then spun and fired out the window. He yelled, "I see you! Don't think you can slip around that way."

If anyone had told Al a week ago that his brother would

be acting as a door gunner for a country house, he'd have never believed it. A lot had sure happened in a short time. He turned and took a first step that nearly tumbled him. The sprained ankle throbbed like someone tapping in time on a bass drum. When he'd been in high school sports, a sprained ankle had always been the most aggravating of injuries. He would try to run or turn quickly, and his body wouldn't be able to keep up with the idea, or at least not without screeching in pain. Then there was always the coach with some dumbass remark, like, "Walk it off."

Al took a cautious step or two. Each time he put weight on the foot, small jolts of electric-like shocks shot up his leg, giving him that coppery taste in his mouth that he associated with pain. He limped through a living room done in hunter green with black walnut trim. He'd never been in her house before, and he wondered whether she or her ex was the hunter. Then he saw a picture of her posed beside a deer with an enormous candelabra of a rack. That explained the gun safe, which had been emptied except for an old muzzle-loading rifle. He realized he knew very little about Fergie. He'd have to keep an eye on Spikey and Nora when Fergie was at his place. For a second, he wondered who was feeding his deer, but the sounds of gunfire coming from inside and outside the house snapped him out of that.

Al made it up the stairs by clutching and pulling upward on to the handrail. He dragged his one uncooperative foot along and, in the process, found a half dozen other sore and aching spots. "Don't ever get old," he muttered to himself, "and fall out of a copter."

At the top of the stairs, he saw Walsh at the end of the hall, looking out a window. That meant Fergie would be at a window facing the other way.

"'Ello, Walsh."

Walsh waved back. "Good to see you too!" But he kept his head facing the window. He raised a scoped rifle, squeezed off a shot, then tucked to one side of the window. "Bastard keeps moving."

Al shuffled into the bedroom opposite Walsh's position. Fergie crouched beside a window, holding a scoped rifle. She wore a brown canvas hunter's jacket with all of its rows of shotgun shell holders filled. It bulked her up considerably. A Winchester Model 12 pump shotgun rested against the wall beside the window.

She jumped up, rushed to him and gave him a brief arm's-length hug. "You're hurt."

They kissed—somewhere between passionate and perfunctory, he thought. Lips, familiar and pressing, hint of urgent tongue that also knew this wasn't the place or time. But there was something else, hesitant and unsure, that cautious familiarity he had only experienced once before—with Abbie. It was a kiss that hid a small lie, or a big one.

She pulled her head back and looked into his face. "What happened?"

"Copter got shot down." He stood very close to her, yet saw nothing in her eyes to alarm him. It was not the time for a chatty moment. He could hear shots coming at them from three directions outside.

"I know that. What about your friend Jaime?"

Al shook his head and looked away.

"Aw, I'm so sorry."

"How are you doing here?"

"Well, the woods are on fire, and that's spreading. Oh, and the sheriff wants to hear from you." She handed him her cell phone. "I can tell you that in my wildest dreams, I never saw this escalating into anything like it has." She shook her head.

"Well, it wasn't helped by Jaime acting like Captain Ahab going after the great white whale, which happens to be Los Zetas in this case. We were just pulling at one thread and getting a bigger thread. He was on some personal vendetta about them encroaching into America, and he may very well be an alarmist, but he was also one of the only ones getting a true picture of the very real danger. Look at the lengths these people go." He waved a hand at the window. He could hear the helicopter sweeping past.

Fergie rushed back to her position and picked up her rifle. "They tried shooting at us from that before, but we were able to keep them at bay."

He punched in Clayton's number then reached for one of the two boxes of 9mm ammo. Holding the phone between his chin and shoulder, he loaded his gun. He took out his smashed cell phone and tossed it on the floor then started shoving a handful of shells into his pocket.

Clayton answered, "How the hell're you people holding out?"

"It's not a perfect world."

"I'm on my way to get the department chopper fired up. I'll be out there in two ticks of a lamb's tail."

Al wasn't sure they had that long. It would be ten, fifteen minutes tops. A short while ago, he had been comparing the department's careful but ploddish ways favorably against the maverick style of Jaime's bunch. But in the current situation, he could have gone for some slap-dash hurry-up.

When Al didn't respond, Clayton said, "Wayon's got his cruiser up to the road outside Ferguson's property, along with three other cruisers, but they're looking at a wall of flames. Someone's spreading the fire on purpose. That way's blocked. No one can get in to help you just yet. The volunteer fire department just pulled up, but they're gonna need a helluva lot more equipment than they've got before they can get through to you. Hang in there. Okay?"

Al hung up and looked toward Fergie. "I think they're building a fire ring around us and will let it do the marching up to the door to finish us off. Reinforcements are here, but can't get through to us for a few minutes, time we may not have."

"Thanks for sugarcoating it, sweetie. We'll have to think of something on our own." She sighed. "You're all cut up and limping. You won't be much use to us crippled. You ought to go see Bonnie at the back door. She's got the first-aid kit. She needed it."

"Why's that?"

"Because she got shot. That's why?"

He made it back down the stairs. He stumbled and nearly somersaulted down the last few steps. "Got to concentrate," he told himself. He felt as tired and beat up as he had ever been.

He waved at Maury, who was firing out the front window. A couple of rifle shots sounded from upstairs. He could hear the crackle and smell the smoke of the approaching wall of fire. *What a jolly time to be alive!* He headed for the kitchen.

Bonnie spun around when she heard him dragging into the room. "Oh, my heavens. You nearly made me crap a biscuit."

"What form of female kung fu is that?"

"The usual. You will never learn our inscrutable ways, grasshopper." She raised a small Smith & Wesson Chiefs Special .38. "This is what my tin-can-shooting daddy would call a belly gun. Daddy was a point-and-shoot kinda guy, and I got the hang of that quicker than most, he said. But right now, I just squeeze off a shot now and then to keep them from thinking that coming through this door is an option. If they get close enough for me to see their bellies, then that's another thing."

"Fergie says you have the first-aid kit and that you were shot."

"Just winged me." She lifted her upper left arm to show the white band of tape and gauze. She pointed at a hole in the door about eye-level to Al. "One of the advantages of being horizontally challenged. Or do I mean vertically challenged? Anyone else would have taken one in the old bean."

"Hey!" Maury shouted.

"What?" Bonnie's voice squeaked up half an octave.

"Why don't you let him watch the back and you come help me, Bonnie?" Maury yelled.

"Because he doesn't have ideas involving his tongue and the back of my esophagus."

"I'm all over that."

"Just like that, you're cured, huh? Hallelujah." She got the first-aid kit off the top of the fridge. She had to really stretch to reach it, and her cute little round belly peeked out from under her blouse.

She gave Al the .38 and positioned him so he could look out the door. Then she tugged off his left shoe and sock.

He felt a warm flush on his cheeks. "Sorry I haven't been able to change clothes in a while."

"Hey, don't sweat it. I'm a nurse. I could tell you tales that would curdle milk that hasn't even come out of the cow yet."

Her movements as she wrapped his ankle were swift and efficient, just as he'd expect from someone who had done it hundreds of times. First some pre-tape, then around and around, back and forth in a crisscross for support. She snipped the last bit of tape. "There."

He handed her the gun then pulled on his sock and shoe. She reached down to help him to his feet, and her blouse parted enough that the better part of her upper body swayed into view.

"Bonnie, did you take off your bra?"

"Yep. When I'm stressed, I kinda like to let the girls roam. Makes me feel free and alive. Tell you the truth, I shave my other parts, too. Makes me feel more naked when I am, not that I might get that chance soon."

"Too much information, Bonnie."

"Aw, come on. Tell me that didn't take your mind off the mess we're in for a second or two there."

He made a practice walk across the room. "Hey, that's really good. I'm not perfect, but I can get around a helluva lot better." Instead of electric shocks like small lightning bolts, he felt a steady low throb, but the foot had a lot more support.

"Did you expect anything less from me?"

"No. Bonnie, you're a pip. Now could you cover me? I'm about to do something very foolish and dangerous."

Both her eyebrows rose, but she stood to one side of the door.

He stretched his legs, tested the taped ankle one more time, and took out his pistol. "See you in the funny papers." He took off out the door in as much of a run as he could muster.

Bullets slammed into the back of the house just to the side of where he'd emerged. He heard another shot fired from close behind him. He glanced back. Bonnie was jogging along right behind him and had just fired her gun in the direction of the shots.

"Bonnie, go back."

"No way. You said to cover you. How can this be more

dangerous than waiting inside the house for the fire to get there?"

He didn't have a snappy answer to that. Besides, he kind of liked the company.

At the corner of the house, he slowed enough to peek around at the front. Fergie's car was never going to sail along the highways again, but he could see no sign of Flavio. Al bent low, painfully, to look for feet under the car. Nope. Flavio had been moving around.

Al scanned all around them then took off at his top speed, which was such that Bonnie nearly passed him a couple of times, but she would drop back to continue as his rear guard. The glimpses he caught of her showed a whole lot of bouncing going on. She was right. It did take his mind somewhere else.

The moment he was past the car he saw movement from the corner of his eye. Flavio stood and reached down to pull a knife from his quiver. The man sure did favor knives over guns, or maybe he had used up the last of his ammo. Al spun and raised his gun but knew he was only going to be "almost" in time.

Bam. Bam.

A tuft of cloth rose at Flavio's shoulder, and a sprinkle of hair flew from where the second shot nearly grazed his skull. Pretty close, but no cigar. From this distance, the .38 Special hollow-point rounds Al had seen Bonnie shoving into that little gun would have plenty of stopping power, especially in a two-pill dose. But she'd missed. The shots clipping by so close did distract him enough for Al to squeeze off two shots of his own, so close on the heels of Bonnie's that they sounded like echoes.

Flavio looked down at the red spreading from two holes six inches apart just above his belt, and his incredulous eyes opened wide. The knife dropped from his hand, and he crumpled to his knees then toppled over on his side.

"What d'you know? It *is* a belly gun," Bonnie said. She lowered her gun.

If she wanted to think she'd plugged Flavio, that was fine with Al. He owed her large for the distraction, and it was no time to rattle her confidence.

"Now get hopping along, Chester." She nodded ahead while she shoved shells into the gun to replace those she'd fired.

He took off, and it took him a few strides to figure out that by "Chester" she meant the limping old guy on *Gunsmoke*, a television show that hadn't aired in many years.

The huffing was getting loud, and he thought it might be from Bonnie then realized he was the one doing the panting. Around them, curls and waves of black smoke lifted from the woods, and flames taller than he was flicked orange-yellow in the sky. The heat from the sun beat down on them, but he could also feel the beginning walls of heat from the fire sweeping across the brown grass all around them. At least the heat took his mind off the growing ache of his ankle that was beginning to feel more like a green break than a sprain.

He headed toward where Eduardo had fallen. In the sky ahead, he could see what looked like lit flares arcing out the side door of a small black helicopter. The copter tilted and came toward them, moving at great speed.

Al ran faster than he thought possible. As he got closer, he saw that Osiel had beaten him to the spot and must have had the same idea. He was bent over Eduardo's body, tugging at the strap to the rocket launcher. At nearly three hundred pounds—quite literally dead weight—Eduardo was not making it easy for Osiel to free the weapon.

Osiel looked up, his brown eyes sparkling with pure hate. At some point he'd gotten too close to the flames, and part of his hair had been burned off. Al could make out the Zeta escutcheon tattooed on the top of Osiel's head—a red and black quartered shield with a Z in the upper right portion. Jaime had said that Osiel was no quitter, that he was obsessive about finishing what he set out to do. Anyone else would have hightailed it out of there already. Osiel epitomized the whole problem with groups like Los Zetas and why they might just win. They had a willingness to hire maniacs, absolute crazies who were incapable of not completing a task. And for what? Not to kill some leader of a competing cartel or a political giant but to do in Maury, a little nobody like Maury.

When Al had almost reached him, Osiel let go of the rocket launcher's strap and raised a pistol. Al zagged left, firing as he moved. Osiel shot back then ducked low. Al zigged the other way, emptying the rest of his clip.

At any other time, Al would have dove to the ground and fired from there, but he was afraid he wouldn't be able to get back up again quickly. One of Osiel's bullets clipped through Al's hair, grazing his scalp. Al whipped back the other direction, each time getting closer.

He could hear the *bam, bam* of Bonnie firing behind him and expected at any second to feel one of Osiel's bullets slam into him. For the very first time he thought of Bonnie and Clyde. Maybe there'd be a song in this someday, if they lived... or didn't.

Al was digging for the spare clip from his pocket when Osiel, sensing Al's gun was empty, stood up straight and used both hands to steady his pistol at Al.

Just as the man started to squeeze the trigger, Bonnie fired again. Osiel's gun swung toward her. Bonnie had sure gotten all Annie Oakley enthusiastic on him all of a sudden. Osiel squeezed off two rounds in her direction. Al used the time to pop his clip, slide a new one in place, and jack a shell into place with the slide.

Al fired and saw a dot appear high in the center of Osiel's chest. He flipped over backward and lay still. Al looked back and saw Bonnie fall to the ground and roll.

The chopper was still zooming toward them. *No time to pause.* He would have to check on Bonnie later. He rushed to Eduardo's body, pushed the corpse to one side, and yanked the rocket launcher clear. He got it to his shoulder just as the copter zoomed down toward him. He lifted the barrel and squeezed the trigger. The rocket whooshed straight up.

Bull's eye.

The rocket flew through the open door and smashed against the back wall of the cabin. Al threw the tube aside, dove flat, and covered his ears.

Boom!

The orange ball of flame lit up the sky as the helicopter exploded. It crumpled as it fell to the tinder-dry field just twenty yards away from where Al had flattened his body to the ground.

That was what should have happened when Eduardo had fired at Jaime's helicopter, but either Cody had been moving too fast or the range had been wrong. Or maybe the rocket had just been a dud. Al glanced at the launcher he had tossed away—a Soviet RPG-7. Hell, he'd been lucky the damn thing had fired at all. Likely as not, it had been stolen out of someone's collection. Yet it was the third one he'd seen in all his years of law enforcement.

He jumped to his feet and ran back to Bonnie. He was glad to see she was sitting up and not just lying there. She had torn a piece of her blouse off and was pressing it to the side of her thigh.

"In and out," she said. "Easy peasy to fix once we get back to the house. Except for one thing."

"What's that?"

"I can't seem to stand up."

He tucked her pistol into his back pocket and his gun in a front one. Then he scooped her up and began to run toward the house as best he could, which wasn't really very fast at all. A club-footed giraffe could have lumbered past him. He glanced back and saw a wall of fire coming their way. He found he could run a little faster after all.

"I got him, didn't I? The big kahuna himself."

"Sure you did, Bonnie," he lied. It seemed important to him at the moment to make her feel good about herself. "Thanks for getting Osiel. He was about to punch my ticket." He huffed, still getting as much speed into the run as he could and glad his ankle wasn't letting him down, though every footstep with that leg now sent pain up him once again like a small lightning bolt.

"Thanks go to you for getting him to stand up and be a target. That hopping around of yours was terrific and quite a bit of fun to watch."

He looked down at her and saw she was grinning past a grimace while holding the scrap of cloth tightly in place. "You won't believe how hard it is to get a man to sweep you off your feet these days." Then she passed out.

CHAPTER TWENTY

A L CARRIED BONNIE THROUGH THE kitchen door, using one hand to keep the reddened damp cloth pressed against the entrance and exit wounds on her thigh. He lowered her to the floor with her back to the wall then grabbed the first-aid kit.

"Fergie!"

"What?" she shouted.

"There's nobody left out there. It's just the fire out there now. I need your help with Bonnie."

Bonnie's eyes fluttered open, and her hands went back to the cloth pressed against her thigh, moving Al's hands away.

Maury stepped into the kitchen. "Really? You got them all? We saw the copter explode. Wow! How'd you do that?" He looked down at Bonnie. "What's wrong with her?"

Fergie pushed Maury to one side and rushed to the sink. She grabbed a couple of the nicer guest towels off the bar beside the sink. She turned the water tap. Nothing. "Figures," she said. "The electric gave out a while ago."

Walsh came into the room. "Did I hear you right? You got all of them?"

Al nodded. "Yeah."

"Most excellent. Your former department usually wins the shooting competitions we have. It's why our guys are trained to go for body first, not head." Walsh leaned against the far wall. He knew staying out of the way was the best way to help at the moment.

"Hat tip goes to Bonnie, really. She was on fire out there," Al said.

Maury had been staring out the door. "We're all going to be that soon enough." He propped Fergie's shotgun against the wall as if glad to be done with it.

Fergie got a bottle of water out of the fridge and dampened one of the towels. She brought them over to Bonnie, knelt, and began to clean the entrance wound. Bonnie started cutting off pieces of tape and preparing a gauze pad. Fergie lifted her hands, and Bonnie squirted half a tube of Neosporin onto the bloody spot then slapped on the gauze pad and taped it into place.

Al admired her efficiency at tending to her own wounds, but there was no time to watch. "Maury. Walsh. You need to come with me and help set some fires."

"What?" Maury glanced to Walsh.

Al went into the living room and got the fire starter, with its extended lighting end, from the fireplace mantel.

Maury had followed him into the room. "You know the front of the house is on fire now, don't you?" Maury pointed toward the door, where the flames were waist high and starting up the sides of the doorway and spreading to the inside walls.

"Yeah, just a matter of time."

"How're we gonna get out of this? We're surrounded."

"The best direction is toward where the fire started, where Jaime's helicopter crashed."

"Really? But how?"

"Come on." Al led Maury back through the kitchen.

Fergie was applying bandages to the back of Bonnie's thigh. "You're lucky. The shot missed the bone."

"That's me. Lucky Bonnie." Her voice had a tiny quiver to it, though.

Al waved for Walsh to come along. Outside, Al rushed to the edge of the grass nearest them and bent to flick the lighter and start the grass on fire.

"What the hell are you doing?" Maury shouted.

Walsh got it, though. He dug a yellow Bic lighter out of his pocket and ran the other direction to begin lighting the grass.

Maury waved his arms. "Hey! Hey! Hey! We don't need more fire. We need less."

Al didn't stop. "The only way out is where the fire is played out or at least dying. It's that way"—he pointed—"where the copter I came in crashed. If we can get a fire to go out and meet that spot, we have a way out. It's our *only* way out."

"Oh." Maury glanced around. He found a small wooden stake from the edge of Fergie's garden and tore off a low strip from his super-sized shirt. He tied that in clumsy fashion around the end. Then he rushed to the nearest burning grass and tried to get the end lighted. It wasn't much, but at least he was trying to help.

"Hey," Maury said, "I saw this in a movie once. It was the sequel of *The Gods Must Be Crazy*. You got this idea from the little bushman, didn't you? Ah, life imitates art once more."

Al almost responded then realized it would have been caustic. He wasn't respecting his brother. That hadn't come all the way back to him yet. This wasn't what Maury was good at, after all, but at least he was making an effort. Al had to give him credit for that. "Need to work on a little grace with that forgiveness yourself," he muttered.

"What?" Maury asked, looking up with a smile from where he'd actually gotten a fire started that was already

196

sweeping away from them and leaving only charred black earth behind.

"I was just thinking that none of us know ourselves as well as we think, do we?"

The wall of flame was racing away from them. Behind that, a higher wall of fire was headed toward them. Al turned to look back toward Fergie's house. Flames were curling around the upper eaves on this side. It wouldn't be long now.

"No. I guess not," Maury said. "Always a work-in-progress and not as much quality material to work with as we thought."

Walsh came back toward them. He shoved his lighter in his pocket, pointed toward the house. "I think we're about done here."

Al nodded. "Yeah. It'll either work or it won't."

They all went back into the house. Al took the two empty guns out of his pockets and put them on the counter. They wouldn't be much use, and he could run better without them. He bent low and scooped up Bonnie.

"My hero," she gushed. Still, despite the brave smile, she was paler beneath her tan. She was making a good effort to shrug off getting shot twice in one day, but she wasn't quite there.

Fergie grabbed bottled water out of the fridge. She gave one to each of them. Bonnie took Al's.

"Hit us, Fergie," Al said.

Fergie twisted the tops of a couple of bottles and poured water over Al and Bonnie's heads, soaking their clothes. She walked around them, splashing water onto any dry spots and making sure their shoes got wet, too. "Okay, you're as good to go as you're going to get with what we have. Next!"

Maury stepped forward.

197

"Always the eager volunteer, aren't you, Maury?" Fergie said.

"Hey, this isn't my first wet T-shirt party."

Fergie sighed and started wetting him down.

Al carried Bonnie outside and started a slow jog toward where Jaime's copter had crashed. At first, his steps were tentative because the ankle was throbbing some. But the wrapping held up, and by gritting past the jolt of each step on that leg, he was able to pick up his pace. He was seeing Jaime and Cody's faces again, and even Bonnie's half-falling out of her wet blouse—with what was inside moving around like happy puppies as he jogged—wasn't blurring the clarity of that mental picture. Then Angel's face crept in. Boy, Al had a lot of regrets about just about everything so far.

Maury rushed up to trot along beside them. He grinned when Al glanced at him in surprise. Maury was moving pretty well for someone who'd been in a hospital bed not too long ago. Actually, it was amazing, considering how feeble his brother had been when they'd brought him out to Al's place. Al glanced back. Fergie and Walsh were jogging behind Maury. They'd left behind their rifles. Walsh had only the pistol at his side. Fergie still wore her brown hunting jacket. They each held a water bottle. Al looked back toward the wall of fire and ran faster, still seeing and remembering more than he liked of Jaime, Cody, Angel, and even Three-legged Bob.

<hr>

Bonnie looked up at Al, watched his face flinch with each jogged step onto the bad foot. That wasn't what was bothering him, though. She didn't much care for the mental wrestling match she saw going on there. He needed a distraction.

She turned to Maury. "Hey, you're the one everyone thinks was getting more ass than a toilet seat. Didn't you ever think about getting serious with any of those ladies?"

Maury frowned, then his expression eased into a smile. "Well, a woman, one who I'd had a one-night fling with thirty years ago, showed up and said she was leaving her husband. She loved him, but they hadn't had sex in eleven years. I don't know what drew her to me. My reputation perhaps? I felt all the old familiar physical attraction for her. We had a pretty hot time of it, even broke some furniture, including the bed. It was as if she were still in her twenties. That reunion went on for two weeks. It could most likely still be going on, but it wasn't what I wanted."

"What do you want? Wouldn't any of the women you were seeing do?"

"Well, of them, Angel would have been the one I would have picked, if I'd been able to make myself do that." He was huffing louder but seemed glad for the chance to chat.

"Why?"

"Because she understood me most... and needed me least."

Al glanced over at Maury. He never seemed all that comfortable with his brother's brash admissions. Walsh looked as though Maury had spouted some sort of riddle. Fergie's mouth had twisted to a wry pucker to one side.

Well, Bonnie had done her distracting best. For at least the space of a few seconds, all of their minds had had a chance to go somewhere else.

⋖◆⋗

The impression that they were running into the gaping jaws of hell began to grow on Al. Smoke billowed in black waves like low, earth-hugging clouds. He tried to think of anything else. His ankle had started to hurt again in earnest, but that wasn't the kind of thing he wanted to take center stage on the dance floor of his tired head.

"Al?" Maury asked. He was coughing occasionally and huffing a bit, but he was keeping up. He took a sip of water and screwed the cap back on, all while having to jog harder now to keep up with limping Al.

"What?" Al looked ahead to the nearing wall of fire and black smoke. He hoped there was enough left in Maury for him to make it.

"Have you ever seen Abbie again?"

Al winced. He hoped Maury wasn't headed toward one of those chats you have when you think you're going to die.

"Well?" Maury insisted.

"Yeah. Once."

"How... how did that go?"

Al took a deep smoky breath and almost went into a coughing fit. When he got his voice back, he croaked, "It was my birthday. I didn't go out much, but I thought I'd take the boat over to The Pier, you know, the place floating out on the edge of lake. I thought I might have a prime rib, maybe feed the fries to the catfish and carp."

"And?"

"She was there. I didn't see her until I was seated, or maybe I'd have left. She came over. I was still toying with the idea of leaving. She said she was doing fine, that the woman with her was her significant other."

"Really? Oh, my God. You turned her into a lesbian, Al?"

"Tender point, but you were dating her last, Maury."

"Oh." Maury paused. "Oh, my God. *I* turned her into a lesbian."

"Men don't turn women into lesbians," Bonnie said. "Although you two are starting to make me consider it."

"That's right," Fergie said. She wasn't panting as much as the rest of them since she jogged regularly. "People are what they are, and it takes some longer to find out what or who that is. But her trying that out after being with you two rhubarbs doesn't surprise me at all. It borders on the cliché."

"You saying my life is a cliché?" Al huffed. He would have waved his arms around them, but had to hold onto Bonnie. "How can you call anything that's happened in the past few days a cliché?"

"I'll grant you that much," Fergie said. It was starting to bug Al how easy it was for her to lope along with those long legs of hers.

"So how'd she look?" Maury asked. "And the girl with her. Was she a bomb?"

"Hey, you guys, I'm right here, with one boob practically falling out of my blouse," Bonnie said.

Maury leaned closer to look, but she waved him away. Al decided to run quietly for a while. Abbie *had* looked terrific. She had a darker tan than he'd ever seen on her, and her auburn hair was cropped short. She'd been wearing a T-shirt over a bikini, and it was clear she'd been spending her time at the gym.

Once, he'd been shot early in his career as a deputy. Sally Bradford had been aiming for her husband, Raymond, who was running out of their house, headed straight for the sheriff's cruiser that had just pulled up. Al got out, Raymond dodged, and the bullet from what used to be Raymond's Ruger .357 hit Al near his waist. The round hadn't torn anything vital, but it had sent him into shock. Next thing he knew, he'd awakened in the hospital. Getting clipped in the side with that bullet was exactly how it had felt seeing Abbie again.

"She sounds playful to me," Bonnie said.

RUSS HALL

"What?" He glanced down at her. It was getting harder for Al to run and talk.

"I mean, she mighta just been kidding around. You know, to get a rise out of you."

"That does sound like her," Maury huffed.

"You think she was just trying to get me to lighten up?" Al's voice grew louder in spite of his having trouble even breathing.

"You do tend to take things seriously," Bonnie said.

"She's not wrong." Fergie still wasn't even breathing hard.

"You think I ought to lighten up right now?" Al's voice grew louder, until it was right on the edge of hysteria.

"Well... yeah," Bonnie said. "It's as good a time as any."

Al couldn't tell if inner anger was stoking him, making him feel warmer, or if it was the flames. He decided to shut up and just run.

The ground felt warm beneath his sneakers, which were soon covered in black soot. The ground was black and smoldering. Ahead, he could see walls of fire moving away as well as toward them. Some flames leaped taller than his head. They had all stopped talking to save their breath for the jog.

He glanced toward Maury, who looked grim but determined. That was a rare look for his brother, but it suited him at the moment. Thick clouds of black smoke rolled across them. The heat increased as they neared the moving walls of fire. Al hoped his sneakers held out. He'd have traded them for asbestos boots if he could.

The water Fergie had poured on them had evaporated enough that Al's shirt began to feel dry and brittle, as if it might burst into flames at any second. Bonnie opened one of the bottles of water and reached up to pour some on his shoulders and splash some on his face. The others were dousing themselves, too. A rivulet of water started to trickle down Al's back, then it dried before it got halfway down. The heat was baking them alive. His steps slowed, and he realized it was because he was gasping for breath. Each intake was raspy hot and didn't contain nearly as much oxygen as it should.

Walsh and Maury had pulled their shirts up to cover their noses. Fergie had a hand over her face and was breathing through her fingers.

He looked back. The house was a single flaming torch, completely engulfed by flames with black smoke rolling in billowing dark clouds upward. Then a wave of black smoke as dense as a dust storm swept over them, and he could see nothing in any direction. He sought to keep going the way he'd been going, but with each step, he grew less sure they were staying true to that. He began to cough, and his eyes watered. The others crowded closer, forming a tight knot, trusting in him.

Al was sure he could no longer tell what direction they were going, or should be going. Everything looked the same in all directions: thick rolling clouds of black smoke billowed over them, with flames showing through in several places. They had gotten close to the back end of the advancing line of fires that they'd started at the house. They were soon slowed to a walk by the pace of their wall of flame. It took a while for the tall grass to burn down to the flat earth, and that stayed hot to their soles. Al wasn't sure if his shoes had caught fire, but they felt as if they had.

Bonnie had pulled her blouse up over her mouth, and she had begun to cough. Al didn't want to tell the others he was no longer sure where they were headed. He could see two walls of flame ahead, but he wasn't sure if that was where they met, where it would be safe to walk once they got through.

"Wait here," he yelled. He took a running jump at the lowest flames ahead, cleared them, and landed in a stretch of tall brown grass. Nope. He spun and ran at a slight angle to get some momentum then leaped back. He barely cleared the flame tips, and when he landed, he had to reach down and pat one smoldering pant leg.

Bonnie was coughing harder. When she could stop, she said, "Can you look and see if I still have eyebrows?"

"Wrong direction?" Fergie asked.

Al coughed. "Right direction, I think. We just need to give it a few more ticks."

"Come on," Walsh said. His eyes narrowed. "Do you really have any idea where you're going?" His voice grew louder as anxiety turned to raw anger. Deep lines furrowed on his brow.

"Well, it's not all that easy. I think I got turned around a little there in all the smoke. But I'm pretty sure we need to go in this direction." Al pointed with a nod of his head.

Walsh frowned. "I hope you're not just making shit up. We're in a tight spot here."

"Really?" Maury said, and it turned into a cough that bent him at the waist. When he managed to stop, he straightened, still red in the face, and began to walk along the edge of the firewall, trying to peer over it.

Walsh was still glaring at Al when Maury called out, "Hey, I think we can get through over here."

Al took off in a jog. Walsh and Fergie both passed him. Maury was right. The fire from both sides had met, and the walls were canceling each other. Al could see blackened tree trunks ahead, along with stands of prickly pear cactus curled into black lumps of coal. Through the

TO HELL AND GONE IN TEXAS

smoke, he caught a glimpse of the blackened hull of the crashed helicopter. They were going to make it.

When the two walls of fire had dwindled to just a foot-high line chewing at the last of the grass, Maury hopped over. Al and the others were right behind him. A black smoldering wasteland spread out before them. The grass was all gone, reduced to soot-covered dirt. The ground was mostly flat and smooth. Most of the smaller shrubs and cacti had been devoured, too. Tree trunks were blackened six to eight feet high, and some had lost their tops.

Al headed toward the helicopter. He didn't want to, but he had to check. They walked across the gentle hills of black that had once been covered in tall brown grass. Not an insect, or lizard, or snake, or scorpion moved, although Al did see the blackened remains of some. One snake, a rattler, was half out of a hole, looking like a crispy twist of licorice. Nothing could have lived through the inferno.

As they neared the smashed remains, Al told Bonnie, "You might want to close your eyes."

"Are you kidding?"

He stepped close while Maury, Walsh, and Fergie hung back. Al peered inside the cockpit. It was empty, as were the seats where he and Jaime had sat. He straightened and looked around. He heard sirens in the distance, out on the road on the other side of where the house had stood. The sound of an approaching chopper came from even farther away.

"Maybe we should just wait here. We're safe now," Fergie said.

Walsh nodded. "Why don't you call?"

Fergie shook her head. "Can't. Lost my cell phone quite a ways back there. Helluva time to be without it."

"Mine went the way of the dodo too," Bonnie said. "The

one time I could use it, though we're probably out of range of the nearest tower anyway."

"What an enormous waste," Maury said.

"What do you mean?" Al wouldn't have minded setting Bonnie down for a moment, but she'd have been filthy in an instant.

Maury waved a hand back toward where the house had been and swept it to the remains of the copter. "All this. All over some petty minor stuff when there are real messes out there, big drugs moving and hardcase sorts doing it."

"Those guys we just tangled with seemed pretty hardcase to me." Fergie took a swig of water, emptying her bottle. She screwed the lid back on and looked about for a place to put the bottle. When she didn't spot any one spot better than another she dropped it to the black dirt with a shrug.

"I mean, Al was saying earlier that Jaime had gotten more than a little like Captain Ahab and that Los Zetas were his white whale." Maury was working himself up. "There's usually a price in such yarns."

"You don't have much room to talk. Hell, you were the one they were after," Walsh said.

They were all tired, hot, and irritated as dammit. But Al still thought that was a raw thing to say. Walsh stepped close to Maury and stood over him in a way that should have intimidated him, even threatened him. Maury stood his ground, frail as he was, and glared up at Walsh. It surprised and pleased Al to see his brother standing up for himself, though he wanted to pull Maury aside and advise him to do it another time, another place.

Walsh balled his hands into tight fists. He shifted his weight, and Al watched his shoulders roll enough to see he was going to hit Maury with everything he had—a haymaker right to Maury's face, from the look of it. Maury, frail as he was, had almost no chance. A darkening red worked its way up Walsh's neck to his tightening jaw, and every muscle in him looked taut enough to explode.

"That's not quite true, Walsh, and you know it," Al said. "They weren't after just Maury. They were after you as well." He knew as soon as the words came out that he should have kept his mouth shut. He should have waited until much later, when they were safe and away. But he also knew Maury's life may well depend on Al saying something.

Walsh spun toward Fergie. His face shifted from open-eyed surprise to eye-narrowing anger. "What have you told them?"

"Nothing. I might've suspected, but you're my partner. I said nothing. You know I would never say a thing."

Al watched Walsh's face the way he would a chess opponent's. Walsh was making up his mind about something, running through all the permutations of how things might come out with the sirens in the distance getting closer and the copter's roar nearing. Walsh tightened his lips and narrowed his eyes.

Al had known for some time what one of Fergie's lies of omission had been. That was why he had stopped pushing Maury about his partner and why he'd been glad Walsh had gone to Fergie's place to help defend it. Walsh had as little reason as anyone to side with the Zetas. But Al would sure have rather waited to push this button. Walsh looked to be on the edge of doing something stupid and rash.

Al had been in well over a hundred fights in his life. He first registered the body language, but it was the eyes he stayed fixed on in the end. They could say anything above the loud talking.

Walsh's face flushed darker. He drew his pistol, pointed it at Fergie, and shot her in the chest.

She flew back and landed flat on the black side of a slope beside the crashed copter. Al's mouth dropped open.

"And you." Walsh spun around, leveling his gun at Al.

"Oh, shit," Bonnie said. Not the best choice for last words, but probably all she had.

Just before Walsh pulled the trigger, Maury leaped in front of Al.

Bam!

The force of the shot slammed Maury into him. Maury's body crumpled slowly to the ground.

"Stupid ass," Walsh said. He'd lowered the pistol for a second. He raised it again.

"You might want to close your eyes," Al said low to Bonnie.

But she already had them pressed shut as tight as she could.

Bam!

Al winced, but he didn't feel where he'd been hit. He looked down at Bonnie. Her eyes snapped open. He looked back up in time to see Walsh drop to his knees then topple over to one side.

Behind Walsh, stretched out on the ground, with a line in the dirt behind him where he'd dragged himself all that way, lay Jaime holding his pistol. He looked up at Al. One eye was swollen shut, and half of his hair had been singed entirely away. Al couldn't tell if he was blinking or trying to wink.

"Now we're even, Al." Then the gun fell from his hand, and Jaime passed out.

CHAPTER TWENTY-ONE

"I 'M GOING TO HAVE TO put you down, Bonnie." Al's words came out as croaks.

"I understand."

Al lowered her beside where Maury lay in a crumpled heap. Tears ran down in wide smears across both his cheeks. Normally, that would have embarrassed him, but at the moment, he didn't give a damn. He lowered himself to one knee.

Bonnie pressed two fingers to Maury's neck. "Al?"

"What?"

"Al?" Her voice got louder and went up an octave.

"What?" he snapped.

"He's alive."

Al's mouth opened then closed. He went on both knees and rolled Maury over. He was out but breathing. Al lifted the bottom of the oversized Longhorn shirt. The bullet was stuck in the front of a bulletproof vest. "How in the hell?"

Fergie moaned.

"Watch him," Al said. "See what you can do."

Bonnie opened her water bottle and started dabbing the liquid onto Maury's face. Al rushed over to where Fergie lay.

Her violet eyes were open. "I think that son of a bitch broke one of my ribs. Maybe two."

Al squatted beside her and tapped her brown hunting

jacket. She also wore a bulletproof vest. "You put one on Maury too. How did you know?"

"I didn't know it would come down to this. I had two and got one onto Maury earlier. Tried to get it onto Bonnie, but it didn't fit. That little gal has some serious boobs."

"I know," Al said. "I mean, I'm just glad Maury was wearing. You saved his life."

She shook her head and looked away. Her shoulders started to shake. Al could think of no reason for it, but she was crying. He picked her up and carried her over to lie beside Maury.

Bonnie moved closer to Fergie. "I'd better have a look. I'm sure getting my money's worth out of nursing school today."

Al went over to Jaime and picked him up.

Jaime's eyes snapped open. "Did you get them, Al?" he rasped.

Al nodded. "Yeah, all of them."

Jaime gave him a tired, feeble grin. Al lowered him to the ground.

"Help me sit up," Jaime said.

Bonnie came over and took his pulse while Al helped him into a sitting position.

"Is Cody okay?" Al asked.

"He's worse off than me but fixable. Where are the rest of my men?"

"Should be here any second."

The sound of the chopper was getting louder. Al looked up and could see the sheriff's insignia on its side.

Maury moaned. Bonnie sighed and went back over to him.

Al asked Jaime, "How the hell did you manage to survive that fire? And the crash?"

"We were out of the helo, right on your heels, Al. But

we landed a ways from where you must've hit. Tell you the truth, I figured you'd hit the ground hard enough you were gonna have to be buried in a pizza box. I'd grabbed a blanket from the emergency kit to half use as a parachute. Didn't help much. I landed in some chaparral, and Cody smashed a pretty big stand of cactus. Broke both his legs, I think. After the helo blew, I knew there'd be fire. The blanket I'd grabbed was a fire-shield blanket. I dragged Cody to a deep enough ditch, got the blanket over us, and the fire swept over us. Mostly." He reached up and touched the singed half of his head. "Sucked the oxygen out of the air, but went by fast enough we got a smoky gulp or two of air almost as soon as it was past. Man, that's dry tinder out there."

The roar of the chopper landing drowned out anything else he might have said.

He pointed across the black soot field, where two black SUVS were racing their way. "Silly bastards'll probably ruin those vehicles, thinking they're saving me when I'm just fine." As soon as he said it, his eyes rolled back in his head, and he slumped over sideways again.

Minutes later, the black vans slid to a stop, sending up roiling black clouds of soot. Men tumbled out, ready for action, weapons pointing in every direction, although there was nothing there but blackened soil. They looked half miffed to find the show over.

They all wore the same black ICE tactical gear but with little individual touches here and there. One had what looked like a Seal knife at the small of his back. Another carried a thin but strong-looking black rope. Most wore their sidearms low on the right hip. Back in the Wild West days of gunslingers, the men to watch out for had been those who wore their pistols like that. The way they all moved, looked about, and carried themselves and their

211

weapons told Al they had all seen military action, Special Forces most likely.

The medic, who wore the thick backpack with Red Cross on it, had his gun right at his belt. It let him run faster, as he demonstrated by leading the way when they rushed to Jaime. The medic dropped to his knees and opened his pack. He cut away Jaime's black cloth and began cleaning wounds, pressing spots, and wrapping a swollen ankle that looked sprained to Al.

In the far distance, Al could see green, so the fire crews had done what they could to keep the fire from spreading. They had to be still at work, though. Smoke rose from several directions.

Jaime woke up and put a hand on the medic's arm. "Enough, Paulo. Go to Cody." He looked toward Al. "Can you go with them?"

Al glanced at Maury and Fergie. Bonnie was doing what she could for them, though she was far from being in perfect shape herself. He got to his feet, hid a little wobble that almost pitched him back down again, and took off as fast as he could along the trail where Jaime had dragged himself.

Al thought he was jogging, but Paulo passed by just walking fast. Two of the other men caught up, and they'd made a trip back to the black vans to get a stretcher.

A dozen yards away, Paulo dropped to his knees. By the time Al got there, Paulo had cleaned Cody's face and had the man's shirt cut open so he could dab at punctures near the neck. He inflated temporary splints onto Cody's legs. One of Cody's eyes was swollen shut and puffed out in a red mound from his face. Al couldn't tell if the young guy was going to lose an eye or not. He remembered how fit and young Cody had looked, cocky even. None of that showed anymore. That didn't bother the other ICE team members. They'd all been to war and seen a lot worse.

Al saw the crumpled silvery fire-shield blanket that had saved their lives. One side was blackened. On the opposite bank of the deep ditch they'd crouched in was a large stand of prickly pear cactus that had been reduced to twisted, gnarled black chunks.

"First time I ever heard of anyone being lucky to land in cactus," Paulo said without glancing up. "Saved his life." He pushed himself upright and started putting things back in his pack, while the other two guys slid Cody onto the stretcher and carried him off at a pace that left Al and Paulo behind.

Paulo fell into stride beside Al. "You okay?"

Al lifted a pant leg and showed him the wrapping Bonnie had done.

Paulo nodded. "Someone knew what they were doing."

"She's a nurse," Al said. "We were lucky to have her along. Turned out to be a pretty handy shooter as well."

Paulo nodded and broke into a light jog. Al faded behind and peeled off as Paulo and the guys carrying the stretcher headed for the vans with Cody. Al made it to the others in time to see Sheriff Clayton climb out of the sheriff's department helicopter. The first of three department cruisers pulled up, trailed by roiling black clouds that caught up to them as they stopped. Deputy Wayon Gallard climbed out of the first.

Clayton pointed at the black SUVs that were driving away. "Where are those guys going with that man?"

"He's one of Jaime's men, the helicopter pilot," Al yelled over to him.

Clayton nodded and walked over to Jaime. The sheriff bent closer, and the two had a whispered exchange. Then Clayton asked loud enough for Al to hear, "You really going to push that button just now, with you not even able to stand on your own?"

The sound of Clayton's raised voice turned Al's head that way. Jaime seemed to try for his blustering in-control expression, but lying on the ground didn't help. His singed face grew a darker red. "Well, I..."

"Don't have much to bargain with, do you?" Clayton gave him a few ticks. When Jaime didn't answer, he said, "Talk to me," and bent closer again.

They kept their voices down, but the conversation got heated. Al enjoyed the slow evolution taking place on Jaime's face. Their sentences were short, terse, with a fair amount of waiting between each one. There was a whole lot they weren't saying, one of those silent slow straining moments like in an arm-wrestling match. Jaime sighed at last and nodded up at Clayton, who still bent over him like a hulking buzzard. At the nod, Clayton stood upright again.

"All right if my men take Cody and me to the hospital?" Jaime asked. He was asking, actually asking, in a respectful way. It was the first time Al had ever heard anything like demure in Jaime's voice.

"I've got ambulances waiting out on the road," Clayton said, "and the STAR Flight copter is on the way."

"If it's all the same with you, Harold, I'd just as soon not climb into a helo again real soon." Jaime winked in Al's direction with his one good eye.

"I hear you on that. You can go, but leave those Zetas men. We'll want to document everything. Then the bodies will be turned over to you. Send your M.E., if you like. I'll need statements from your people, too, especially one from you about what went down with Walsh. I'll give you copies of everything I gather. This will be your show after all. But my men will handle it. Okay?"

Jaime hesitated. His beat-up face shifted into a frown, one that had nothing to do with pain. Al sensed a tension between the two men he couldn't explain.

Jaime's good eye moved left then right, and he seemed to be mulling something over. Then he nodded slowly and smiled. "Okay. Okay, Harold."

Jaime's men helped him to his feet. One of them gave him an ICE ball cap. He seemed to think about that then tugged it on. He took a step, faltered, and nearly fell. One man got one of Jaime's arms over his shoulders and another took the other side. Jaime's legs dragged slightly as they headed away. Al thought there seemed to be a lot of macho silliness going on. Clayton chuckled.

The rest of the black-dressed ICE crew climbed into the black SUVs. They zoomed out of sight across the smoking black fields, leaving the sheriff and his department to handle the cleaning up of the mess.

As soon as they were gone, Wayon came running over to Al, grinning like a possum that had just found the pie. "Whoee. Clayton told me I'd be replacing the most piss and vinegar detective he'd ever had on staff, and he wasn't wrong." He raised a hand to slap Al's shoulder but quickly lowered it.

Al figured he probably looked like a solid bruise by now.

Clayton knelt beside Fergie. They were talking too softly for Al to hear.

Then Clayton stood, dusted off his knee, and ambled up to Al, thumbs in his belt. "Gonna need the usual paperwork, Al."

"Sure. First thing after I get these people taken care of." He nodded to Maury, Fergie, and Bonnie.

Bonnie wiggled the fingers of one hand up at the sheriff.

"Hell, of course. You, too. You oughta see yourself. You

215

look like the last chapter of 'What's the Use.' You probably need a check-up from the neck up while you're at it. Damnedest bit of tomfool running around I can imagine. What the hell, Al? It's usually just the young pups like Wayon here who think they're bulletproof."

"Oh, I don't think that, sir. I don't think anything like that," Wayon said. He was still young enough to think anyone who mentioned his name was talking about him.

"Well, all I can say is you took out some of the baddest Zetas who ever waltzed into my... this county." Clayton looked back toward where Fergie's house once stood.

"I have to give a lot of credit to Bonnie there. She got two of them, and with a Chiefs Special." The stretched truth didn't hurt anything, Al figured. It was the way she'd remember it.

Wayon's gaze moved to her, and he raised his eyebrows.

"It's a belly gun, so guess where I got them?" she said.

"Really?" Clayton used a forefinger to tilt the front brim of his hat up an inch. "Well, you must be one of them West Texas gals. I hear they eat mountain lions for breakfast."

"Oh, please don't talk about food. I believe I *could* eat a lion just now."

Wayon turned his face away and put a hand over his mouth, but Al heard the chuckle. The roar of the STAR Flight copter landing drowned out any response Clayton might have made.

Once it had settled into a steady whopping, ready to take off again as soon as loaded, Al told Clayton, "I'm the least banged up. I can ride to the hospital with you and dictate a statement on the way. These three will be all STAR Flight can handle."

Clayton nudged Al toward the department copter. "The crime scene crew and M.E. are on their way, and I've got twenty deputies clocking in for some overtime."

Al nodded toward his ragtag little group. "Let me make sure they get off."

Clayton waited until Fergie, Bonnie, and Maury had been loaded onto the STAR Flight helicopter, and it had lifted up again and roared toward Austin. Then he started to move Al toward the department copter.

"You stay here, Wayon," Clayton said. "Mark where the bodies fell and take pictures. Get as many shots as you can of Walsh. There's going to be plenty of squawking from city about him."

"You said that after we're done here this was going to be an ICE operation, sir. Why so?"

"Wayon, you'll find we'll need those fellows again. Don't care much for it myself, but it's the way things are, have become. They're going to be around because the problem's still around, and it's likely to only get worse. So the more we can butter their bread now, the better off we're gonna be down the road. You hear?"

"I understand." Wayon didn't sound convinced.

"Look at it this way," Clayton said. It was rare, almost nonexistent, for him to climb on a soapbox and preach, but Al caught enough of a shift in his tone to brace for it. "I'm all for taking care of our own, but even I have to admit to limits now and then to what we're capable of, what we're willing to do. What's happened here is a little scrape at a scab. Some blood flowed. That's just the beginning. You take on these Zeta guys, and you're going to get a whole gush of rushing hot-blooded types, and I mean the kind of folks going around gutting and doing way more than just decapitating people. I haven't been fast or easy about coming to this view myself. There are no rules of conflict with these folks. None at all. They don't go beyond the limits, because they don't even know there *is* a limit. It's the kind of thing I want as few people in this county

217

knowing about or having to experience as possible. Now, if Jaime and his bunch want to go around hiring the sort of people able to stand up to this breed of mob, well, he's going to get mavericks, half-cocked crazies, and the lot. Truth is, they're around, and this may be the best use of them. God bless men like Jaime and all they're doing. It's a war, and he and his kind want to be on the front line. I say let them. You don't want to expose your soul to the kind of battles that are gonna happen between the likes of these two forces. Jaime wants nothing less than that, to be on the front line in it, and my hat's off to him. Got it?"

Wayon swallowed and nodded. Al wasn't sure if Wayon did get it, but Al knew Clayton was done talking, after the longest tirade Al had ever heard from him, and the person he was seeking to convince wasn't Wayon. Clayton faced one of those moments when history was mounted on a hinge, and he stared inevitable change in the cold dark eye. He was trying to convince himself.

Clayton's face had clanged shut like a steel gate, and his eyes showed little emotion as he panned across the charred wasteland around them. Al couldn't tell if he'd succeeded in convincing himself of anything. But then, Jaime was gone, and Clayton still stood here, in his county, doing what he could to enforce the law and perhaps even shelter a few innocents.

CHAPTER TWENTY-TWO

THE CAR WOVE THROUGH THE trees, showing flickers of itself between tree trunks and hanging limbs until it pulled into the open and eased up in front of Al's house. The deer gathered around him looked up from the deer pellets he was scattering for them. They watched Fergie climb out of her car, then they looked at Al.

"She's okay," he said. That was a tiny stretch. He'd seen that hunting photo of her with the trophy buck.

When Nora and Spikey were born and had staggered out of the woods on wobbly legs as two wet dark twins with bright white spots, their mother came out and licked them over. Then she took them over to Al, who stood at the feeding spot with a bucket. She'd let the fawns come up to him, as if to let them know he was okay, that he could be trusted. He supposed they understood when he cleared someone with them. Maybe they didn't, but what the hell.

Fergie walked with those lanky controlled strides that always made Al think of a panther, or some other large feline predator. He emptied the rest of the bucket and went over to hug her.

She winced. "Gently," she reminded him. She still had her chest wrapped because of the two cracked ribs.

The hug she gave back was as gentle, since Al's torso was still wrapped, too. Their hug reminded him of the way porcupines are said to make love—very carefully. His hand slid across the small of her back.

She stepped back and raised an eyebrow. "Really? I'm not carrying." She didn't ask why he'd checked. Didn't need to. Their eyes locked for a second.

"Just practicing, in case I have to take a job as airport security."

Pink spots appeared on her cheekbones, then she gave a light shrug. "Sure. We'll go with that."

They were on what Al liked to think of as an "advanced level of understanding." That was a phrase he'd come up with back when he was interrogating suspects and wanted to let them know he knew enough that it would be best not to hold back and make the session longer than necessary.

She shook her head and turned to take in the new paint on the front of the house and the repaired door. "The place looks good as new. I'd try to hire away your handyman, but I don't have as much left to work with. That guy is a wizard. Look what he did in just a week."

"You had your homeowner's insurance same as me, didn't you?"

"Yeah, but now to decide: rebuild or travel? After a week of talking with Internal Affairs and trying to sound as surprised as they are about Walsh, the road's looking pretty good."

"Come on inside. It's the hour when retired people have a libation. You're retired now, aren't you?"

"Yeah, I put in the paperwork. It'll be official soon enough. I thought you didn't keep any liquor in the house."

"Bonnie picked up some champagne, said we should all celebrate being alive."

"Sounds like her, and she's probably got a point. Is she still staying here?"

"Until Maury gets well enough to go about on his own.

He was pretty frail to begin with, and this last frolic just about did him in. She has managed to keep him on a tight path toward being a perfect gentleman. I hardly recognize him this way."

"So just like that, he's cured?"

"No, but it's a step in the right direction for Maury. It probably doesn't hurt that he thinks she shot a couple of badasses who needed shooting. But she's a regular lion tamer, and I believe he's becoming genuinely more respectful."

"We'll see."

"Hope springs eternal. At least he hasn't once asked her if she wants to charm his one-eyed snake."

"She may well have done what no woman has done before."

"It's progress. He never listened to me before."

"I'm glad you and Maury are talking again. What do you talk about?"

"Everything. We have a lot to catch up on." He led her into the kitchen.

Outside the window, Bonnie and Maury sat on the deck at opposite sides of a table with a Scrabble board between them. They each had a stemmed glass half-full of pale bubbling liquid. Maury was bent over, studying his letters. Bonnie saw them in the kitchen and waved.

The champagne bottle was open in an ice bucket in the sink. Al got two stemmed glasses down from the cupboard. He poured her a glass and handed it to Fergie.

He was pouring his glass when she asked, "What will we toast?"

"How about honesty among friends?"

She lowered her glass and set it on the table. "If you have cards you think you need to play, play them."

"Well, there were a couple of pieces to the puzzle I

was having trouble reconciling. They didn't fit. You're a detective. You know how that is."

"*Was* a detective. Now I'm retired... like you. What are you talking about?"

"I think you know."

"Enlighten me."

He took a small sip of his champagne. "Go ahead. Taste it. It's pretty good. Honesty, remember?"

"Where're you headed, Sherlock?"

"The black book. I wondered why you'd overlooked it, left it in Maury's room. It wasn't the many women you wanted me to see. It was one of the very few male names. Walsh. What was your partner's name and address doing in Maury's book? It could mean only one thing. He was the one with the connections to get product sent to Maury, the patsy. Maury would have thought it an easy way to get by, clever even, and it wasn't like he was dealing in big drugs. Walsh was actually the one unloading the stuff. I'm sure you would've noticed if his finances were gradually a little better than they might once have been."

"All right. You got that far. What else are you putting on the table?"

"The pieces that didn't fit."

"Such as?"

"Well, there's someone slipping Maury Viagra in his GeriGade. Lab results came through. That was the medium."

"So? What's your point?"

"He has a bad heart. It's why he was in that place. It was an obvious, heavy-handed, and slightly ironic way to call attention to what he was involved in. He was almost done in by Viagra."

"You think I did that?"

"I know you did it. No way to prove it. You're too smart for prints."

"You know I didn't want to hurt him. I would have never wanted that."

"But it really wouldn't get my attention if he didn't land in a hospital as a possible homicide, would it?"

"I'll grant you that. But he is alive, Al."

"Noted. He's alive. And I can't say in those early times if I wouldn't have been tempted to do that to him myself."

"But just not talking to him was enough, wasn't it?"

"I made it be enough. There was a time I might have killed him. I thought about it, planned it, but made myself stand down." Al gestured at her glass. "Go ahead. Drink."

Fergie shrugged, picked up her glass, and took a tiny sip. "It is quite good."

"Then there was the syringe attempt at the hospital. The foiled attempt."

"He's clearly a lucky fellow."

"Yeah, sure. Lucky. The shotgun blasts from a boat with deer slugs came next. By then, Maury was marked as a mysterious character who knew something. Well, all he really knew was that Walsh was the one he turned the packages over to when they arrived. A simple gig, really. Get mail, take out the shells, and pass it on. But Maury wasn't talking to anyone, and Walsh had no reason to do him in. So I began to think the attempts on Maury, all of which failed, weren't to kill him but were made by someone else to stir up interest in Maury's silent partner. With your hair up, you could easily have been the man with the syringe. And I think I've even seen the shotgun now that was used to shoot at this house. It probably burned to nothing in the fire at your place."

Fergie knocked back the rest of her champagne and set the empty glass back on the table. He waited for her to speak. But she outwaited him. So he said, "You had a partner. It's the code of such relationships that you couldn't rat Walsh out. Plus, you liked the guy, genuinely liked him, no matter what. But what if you made it look like someone was trying to kill Maury? That might swing the spotlight around to Walsh in time, and you wouldn't have to be the one to drop a dime on him."

"Look, I lost a house here."

"And a partner. You said you'd retire when you'd wrapped up a few loose ends. Walsh was that loose end, wasn't he?"

She turned her head and watched Bonnie and Maury both laughing at something. The sun was heading for the horizon behind them, bathing the surface of the lake in an orange glow.

He poured a dollop of champagne into her glass. She looked down at it, maybe deciding if it was half full or half empty.

Her head lifted and she gave him a direct stare. "Where do we go from here? What... what are you going to do with these insights, this information?"

He didn't say anything.

"You think you've been played. Used. Don't you?"

"Of course I do."

"Did you think you were in love?"

"I was mighty infatuated for a stretch there."

"You should get out more, Al. You stay off by yourself and away from intimate contact for that long, and that sort of thing is gonna happen."

"Someone's liable to come along and play me like a cheap violin. Right?"

"The way it was supposed to work was Maury would be the one to give Walsh up. It would work better for me that way." She drained her glass again.

"Right. But he didn't. He had caught that same crap about partners we all believe, and worse, he got it from me. So he's as complicit as you. Did you have any idea this would spin off and send that killer Zeta crew after us?"

"No. I thought Walsh would pop out of the rabbit hole sooner than he did. I realize now that you knew earlier on than you're saying. Why didn't you point him out?"

"Hubris. First of all, I thought I was up to protecting Maury—and you—and that it would all run its course. I didn't count on Jaime having someone close to him who was bent as your partner, Walsh."

"The best laid plans, eh? Once things got rolling down the hill, they kind of got away from us."

"They did indeed. We all of us have somewhere we'd rather not go, to hell and gone at that. This took us there."

"I'll ask again. What are you going to do with what you know?"

He hesitated then shrugged. "I guess the same as Clayton. Nothing. He knew. Didn't he? That's what he talked to you about when we were still out there on that sooty field. This particular mess was pitched to him wrong from the get-go. All he wanted was leverage to get his county back. He has an odd sense of justice at times. I guess I picked that up from him. You did make sure Maury was wearing a vest. That saved his life. Way I see it, we're square."

She let out a long slow breath. He could see the tension drain from her like sand pouring from her heels.

Al put his glass beside hers and filled them both to the top. "So what're you going to do now that you're retired?"

"Oh, travel maybe. There are a lot of places I haven't seen."

Travel. Would he travel with someone like Fergie? Could

225

he trust her? Could she trust him? He was following that line of thought out to its logical conclusion when it faded like an ellipse. "Not stay here?"

"No. There's nothing for me here."

"That's what I thought."

"That's what you knew."

"Back at my place that night, were you just throwing me a bone?"

"It was the other way around, if I remember right." She grinned and picked up her glass.

"What about me?"

"Oh, you need something. But it's not me. Maybe someone you can go fishing with." She glanced outside.

The sun slipped over the tops of trees in the distance, and it grew suddenly darker. Maury and Bonnie began gathering up the Scrabble pieces and putting them in a box.

"Plus you'll probably let Maury stay here now," she said. "You might find that enriches both of your lives."

"Perhaps."

"Tell me. You're a little relieved, aren't you?"

"Some," he lied.

"Didn't have a ladder, did you?"

"Oh, I have a ladder."

"All the media coverage I caught sure paints Jaime as the hero of the day. He and his men. And that's not all. I tried to check on any of the federal records about Maury. Any mention of him is gone. It's like he never existed at all, not even a shadow of a ghost."

"That's Clayton's doing. It's what Jaime wanted, too. They must've had quite a chat and come to terms. If the Zetas want to take on anyone, Jaime would just as soon wear the bull's-eye, and Clayton would just as soon it happen someplace other than in his county. It also takes the spotlight off Maury, we hope. Part of the deal was Maury had to give the money away."

"How'd Clayton know there was money?"

"He's Clayton."

"Give it away to whom?"

"Charities. Doctors Without Borders. The Red Cross. I helped him pick out a few, watched him turn the cash into certified checks, and mailed them off myself."

"What will Maury do for money?"

"Hell, I feed the deer, I can feed Maury."

"This mess sure skidded sideways from what I thought would happen. I hadn't planned on Walsh getting killed in the bargain."

"Clayton's the one who had to start the city's internal affairs in the right direction, and they found plenty enough. Isn't that what you wanted in the end? Forget about Walsh. The man tried to kill us all."

"There's that. I really didn't mean to hurt Maury, either."

"I suppose what doesn't kill him makes him stronger. But at our age, when the advanced years keep advancing faster and faster, you've got to be careful."

"You've always been careful, Al. Too careful. Maybe it's time you cut loose and do half the crazy stuff your brother has."

"Perhaps. Perhaps you're right. Or maybe I'll just live vicariously and take copious notes."

"That does sound more like you. I know you try very hard, but I'm not sure you're even capable of romantic love anymore. You're fine with the deer and such, but the inside of you must be solid scar tissue."

He nodded. "That's what it feels like most times."

"I don't know, though, Al," she said. "You seem to be at peace with yourself for the first time."

"I believe I am. I believe I am at that."

She raised her glass. "To honesty."

They clinked to the toast and were drinking when Maury and Bonnie barged in, chattering like a couple of excited monkeys on banana day.

OTHER BOOKS BY RUSS HALL

Thrillers

Island

Wildcat Did Growl

Talon's Grip

World Gone Wrong

Mysteries

The Blue-Eyed Indian

Bones of the Rain

South Austin Vampire

No Murder Before Its Time

Black Like Blood

Goodbye, She Lied

Westerns

Bent Red Moon

Bullets in the Wind

Three-Legged Horse

Young Adult Sci Fi

Inside Jupiter

ACKNOWLEDGMENTS

I wish to thank Joann Dominik and the rest of the Red Adept Publishing staff.

Also, huge thanks to my early manuscript readers, Stewart Emery and Tim Moore.

ABOUT THE AUTHOR

Russ Hall is author of fifteen published fiction books, most in hardback and subsequently published in mass market paperback by Harlequin's Worldwide Mystery imprint and Leisure Books. He has also co-authored numerous non-fiction books, most recently *Do You Matter: How Great Design Will Make People Love Your Company* (Financial Times Press, 2009) with Richard Brunner, former head of design at Apple and *Now You're Thinking* (Financial Times Press, 2011), and *Identity* (Financial Times Press, 2012) with Stedman Graham, Oprah's companion.

His graduate degree is in creative writing. He has been a nonfiction editor for major publishing companies, ranging from HarperCollins (then Harper & Row), Simon & Schuster, to Pearson. He has lived in Columbus, OH, New Haven, CT, Boca Raton, FL, Chapel Hill, NC, and New York City, moving to the Austin area from New York City in 1983.

He is a long-time member of the Mystery Writers of

America, Western Writers of America, and Sisters in Crime. He is a frequent judge for writing organizations.

In 2011, he was awarded the Sage Award, by the Barbara Burnett Smith Mentoring Authors Foundation—a Texas award for the mentoring author who demonstrates an outstanding spirit of service in mentoring, sharing, and leading others in the mystery writing community. In 1996, he won the Nancy Pickard Mystery Fiction Award for short fiction.